RARE

RIKKI'S AWAKENING

DAWN SULLIVAN

Published by Dawn Sullivan

Cover Design: Dana Leah- Designs by Dana

Photographer: Shauna Kruse-Kruse Images & Photography

Model: Chandra Holt

Editors: CP Bialois and Jamie White

Language: English

For Kathy. My friend, my sister, my partner in crime since kindergarten.

RARE: RESCUE AND RETRIEVAL

EXTRACTIONS

Angel: RARE alpha, wolf shifter, strong telepathic

Nico: Angel's right-hand man, wolf shifter, telepathic, has the ability to see glimpses of the future

Phoenix: Human turned wolf shifter, telepathic, complete badass, loves anything that goes boom

Rikki: Human, kick ass sniper, touches objects that others have touched and gets visions of the past, present, and sometimes the future

Jaxson: Wolf shifter, telepathic, RARE's technology expert, dream walker

Trace: Black panther shifter, telepathic, badass sniper

Storm: Wolf shifter, strong telepath, has the ability to see into the future

Ryker: Bear shifter, telepathic

Flame: Telepathic

Bane: Wolf shifter, telepathic (other gifts unknown at this time)

Sapphire: Wolf shifter, telepathic, has the ability to see into the future (other gifts unknown at this time)

R ikki cried out in agony as fire raced through her veins. Her back arched off the bed, and she dug her fingers into the stark white sheets she lay on. A thin layer of sweat coated her skin and tears streamed down her face as she felt an inferno of heat ravage her from within. She struggled to figure out what was happening while the pain slammed through her.

"What's going on? What's wrong with her?" Rikki heard a soft voice question urgently right before she let out another loud, piercing scream. Fear consumed her as it felt as if her body was being turned inside out.

"She's trying to shift," another voice said harshly. "Dammit, Angel is gone on a mission. Hurry! You need to get Chase. We need an alpha here, now!"

Distantly, Rikki realized she recognized one of the voices. Doc Josie was the doctor for the White River Wolves, which meant she must be in their hospital. That would make sense with the amount of pain she was in. It seemed like her body had a mind of its own as she once again arched up, her body twisting and turning in agony, almost throwing her off the bed. She cried out when a sharp jab of pain sliced up her spine, her chest heaving as she fought to bring air into her lungs. Groaning loudly, she turned on her side and curled into a ball, wrapping her arms tightly around her legs. Her breath came out in short spurts as she tried to pant through the pain. It was a struggle to open her eyes, but she finally managed.

The bright lights in the room blinded her and she looked around wildly. What was going on? What was wrong with her? She had never felt this kind of intense agony before in her life.

"Stop this, Rikki," the doctor ordered, taking a step closer to the bed. "Get control of yourself."

Rikki gasped, closing her eyes to block out the light. "Hurts," she managed to snarl, followed by what sounded like a low growl. *What the hell?* Shaking her head, she spat, "The light, it hurts. Shut it off."

"I'll get it." There was that soft voice again. Rikki's brows furrowed in confusion when a deep, acrid scent hit her. What was that smell? As the scent grew stronger, she opened her eyes and her gaze connected with a frightened nurse standing in the doorway. The woman stood immobile, clutching a clipboard tightly to her chest.

"Thank you," Rikki rasped quietly, not wanting to scare her any more than she obviously already had. Slowly turning her head to look at Doc Josie, she took a deep breath, trying to understand what was going on. Suddenly, her eyes widened and met the doctor's in terror when a sharp pain slammed up the back of her neck and into her skull. Her gums ached, and she swore when she accidentally bit into her tongue.

"You need to calm down," Doc Josie ordered as she placed a gentle but firm hand on Rikki's arm. "The change will come so much easier if you just let your wolf take over. Stop fighting her, Rikki. All she wants to do is protect you."

Wolf? Rikki thought as she fought the urge to throw up. Squeezing her eyes tightly shut against the pain in her head, she moaned when she felt something digging into the palms of her hands. Glancing down, her eyes widened in shock as she saw the claws that had sprouted from her glove-covered fingertips.

"Rikki, look at me," Doc Josie ordered, grasping one of Rikki's hands. "You need to calm down. You are going to hurt yourself."

A growl erupted from deep within Rikki's chest, and she turned to glare defiantly in the doctor's direction. "You don't get to tell me what to do," she spat angrily. Ripping her hand from the doctor's, Rikki snarled lowly, refusing to bow down to the other woman.

"No," a deep voice interrupted, "but I do." Swinging her head around, Rikki curled her top lip up, baring her teeth at the male. Chase Montgomery, the alpha of the White River Wolves, stood just inside the doorway, watching her calmly.

Rikki froze when she felt his energy begin to build throughout the room as he pushed his power in her direction. She knew he was trying to help, but it just pissed her off. "Stop it!" she demanded loudly, growling lowly at him. She would not allow him to control her. She would cower down to no one, dammit.

"Enough," Chase commanded roughly, taking a step closer to her. Against her will, Rikki whimpered in pain and confusion when Chase pushed more of his power her way. She had never felt anything like it before. "You will not fight me, Rikki. I am your alpha and you will stand down," he demanded. "Do you understand?"

Shivering in fear at the sheer power radiating off the formidable male, Rikki collapsed back onto the bed, sobs tearing from her throat. "What's going on?" she whispered raggedly. "What are you doing to me?"

Rikki stiffened when she felt a hand stroke down her long, dark hair gently, soothingly. "It's going to be okay," Chase promised her in a quiet, comforting voice. "I'm here now. You are going to be just fine."

Shivering again, Rikki cried softly as the pain continued to ravage her body. "It hurts. It hurts so fucking much. Please, make it go away. Please." She had never felt so weak and vulnerable before, and she hated it. She'd been on her own since she was a child. She'd gone through hell and back and survived, but she had never been in the kind of agony she was now, not even when she took a bullet meant for Nico.

As Rikki lay there fighting the need to lash out at someone or something, she suddenly felt the pain slowly start to ebb away, her body once again becoming her own. After several minutes, she opened her eyes and whispered softly, "I don't know what you did, but…thank you."

Chase continued to gently stroke her hair as he told her, "Your wolf just wants to protect you, Rikki. One of these days, you are going to have to let her. For now, I have pushed her back down and told her to wait. There is nothing to be afraid of. Your wolf would never harm you. She's a part of you. To harm you, would mean she would harm herself."

"My wolf?"

Chase's eyes narrowed, his hand coming to rest lightly on her shoulder. "Do you remember what happened?"

Did she? Rubbing a hand over her face, she tried to recall how she had ended up in the hospital this time. It seemed as if it were becoming a recurring habit. One she needed to break. "It's all so foggy," she admitted finally.

Chase sighed deeply as he ran a hand roughly through his dark hair. "How much do you recall?"

Frowning, Rikki's hand drifted down to cover her neck and she stiffened, her eyes widening in horror. "I was shot. Again. This time in the neck."

Chase nodded. "Yes."

"I was dying."

"Yes, you were," he agreed quietly. "Jinx and Angel saved you."

"Saved me how?" Rikki asked in confusion. Even though she could remember being shot, everything after that was a blur.

"The only way they could." There was silence, and then, "They cheated death by turning you, Rikki. You are now one of us."

One of them? That could only mean one thing. Letting her eyes close in exhaustion, Rikki whispered, "I'm not ready to hear anymore, Chase."

"You don't really have a choice, Rikki. Your wolf won't wait much longer."

"Please, not yet. I'm not strong enough. The pain, it's excruciating." She started to shake as waves of coldness began to rack her body. She felt so weak, so sick.

"The first shift will hurt," Chase agreed quietly as he pulled the blankets up around her shoulders, tucking them tightly around her. "Once you get through that first shift, though, it will be so much easier. You and your wolf will work together. You won't be fighting each other. You are very blessed to have her with you, Rikki. To share a soul with her." Running his hand gently down her hair one last time, Chase said softly, "Sleep now, little one. Sleep."

Burrowing deep into the covers, Rikki sighed as the last of the pain finally receded. Utterly exhausted, she let herself drift off to sleep, a pair of dark brown eyes flashing through her mind. Right before she went under, she murmured, "Jeremiah."

———

CHASE WATCHED as Rikki slipped back into a deep sleep before walking over to sit in the chair by the window. The young woman had been through so much since she and her team came to help his pack the year before. First, shot and taken prisoner by the General's men. Then, shot again a few months later. A fatal shot that required she be turned into one of them or she would have died. After that, they almost lost her to one of the General's assassins who was able to slip into people's minds and manipulate them into doing whatever they wanted. That bitch Ashley had Rikki close to giving up on life. Luckily, they'd been able to track her down and eliminate the problem before Rikki actually left this world for the next. Since then, she'd been in a deep, healing sleep. No matter what they did, they were unable to wake her. Until now.

"What do we do?" he asked Doc Josie quietly.

"We wait," she said, her eyes on Rikki in concern.

"You think she will go back to wherever she was before? Refusing to wake again?"

The doctor shook her head thoughtfully. "No. I've never dealt with anything like this before, but if I had to guess, I would say Rikki's wolf won't allow her to drift away from us again."

"I agree."

"I think it's important to have her team near her right now. The people she considers family. She's going to be frightened and will need all of the love and support she can get for a while to help her through the transition from her human world to our shifter one."

Chase nodded, taking out his phone and sending a quick text. "RARE is on a mission, but should be back in the next couple of days. Phoenix stayed behind because Serenity is close to giving birth. I'll get them both in here."

"Sounds good. I want someone with her at all times, just in case..."

"You don't have to worry about her being alone," Chase interjected. "I'm not going anywhere." He knew what the doctor was thinking. Rikki's wolf was strong, and Rikki had no idea how to control her. They didn't need anyone getting hurt on accident. He had a pack to protect, and that pack included Rikki. She was one of his wolves now, and he would keep her safe, even if it was from herself.

2

Jeremiah Black rubbed a hand over his face in exhaustion, ignoring the conversation going on around him. He really didn't give a shit how much the little prick in the corner wanted to jerk off to the image of one of the prisoners they had in Virginia. Or how another one of the guards thought they should take turns beating a powerful lion shifter they'd captured the month before, because he refused to bow down to anyone no matter what they did to him. Then, there were the rumors of the General's death and Ebony's takeover. Speculation on how it happened, and what to expect now. He didn't have to wonder what happened. He knew. He was there when RARE infiltrated the facility he was stationed at. He'd heard the gun go off. Heard Ebony was the one who pulled the trigger. He'd also seen Jaxson, a RARE team member, tear out the General's throat. Yeah, he knew it all, but right now he didn't give a fuck about any of it.

His mind was consumed with thoughts of his beautiful

mate, who was currently in the hospital at the White River Wolves compound in a deep sleep, from what he'd been told. What the hell did that mean, anyway? Was it similar to a coma? Angel told him Rikki wasn't in any pain. That's what mattered. But... what had happened to her? The thought of his strong, courageous mate, fighting for her life while he was working for the bastard who hurt her in the first place had him wanting to rip out the heart of every soldier in the room with him. The General's men, now Ebony's.

Gritting his teeth, Jeremiah glanced around the small area that he and five other guards were crammed into. They each had a cot, a tiny dresser with two drawers to keep their clothes in, and that was it. They shared a bathroom that was just big enough to walk in, turn around, and sit your ass on the toilet. Or take two steps to the right and climb in the shower. Lucky for him, none of the other men seemed to think cleanliness was important, so he never had to fight for a shower. His shifter genes protested the stench that filled the room he had to sleep in with the filthy bastards, though. And they thought shifters were the animals.

"Yo, Jer, what do you think of that little hottie in Virginia? You know, the feisty one with the long red hair."

What Jeremiah thought was that he wanted to punch the little fucker in the face. That poor little fox was hurting, no matter how sassy she might be to them. And the betrayal in her gaze when she looked at him with those large amber eyes was like a punch in the gut every single time he saw her. He knew she couldn't understand why a shifter would work for someone like the General. Unfortunately, he couldn't tell her the real reason he was there.

All he could do was treat her the same way he did all of the other prisoners he came into contact with. With indifference. If he acted as if he gave a damn about any of them, even in the slightest, the other guards would pounce on him. He couldn't afford to have that happen. He'd worked his way too deep into the organization to have his position second guessed by anyone. So, with a shrug, he said, "She's okay. Not really my type."

"Not your type? Shit, man, she's fine!"

"Exactly what is your type?" Jerret Kyle, one of the other guards, asked. "I've worked with you for months now, but as far as I know, you haven't dipped your dick into any pussy since I've known you. What, you prefer guys or something?"

Jeremiah stood and walked over to him, staring down at him, his face a hard, cold mask. Jerret was a cruel son of a bitch. From what Jeremiah had been able to find out, he'd been with the General's organization for close to three years now. He loved to mess with the prisoners — shifters and psychics both; he didn't care. They were all beneath him in his opinion. "Do I look like I prefer guys?" he growled, getting right up in the other man's face. Hell, he didn't care what anyone's sexual preference was. He had a female cousin who was bisexual, and he fully supported her. Would kick anyone's ass who spoke out against her. But he couldn't let these bastards know that.

Jerret's lips peeled back from his teeth in a snarl. "No, but since you aren't out there getting laid, I figured there must be something wrong with ya."

"What's it to you who I fuck?" Jeremiah questioned, raising an eyebrow.

Jerret was quiet for a moment, then threw his head

back and laughed. Clapping Jeremiah on the shoulder, he said, "Just giving you shit, man. Thought maybe something had to be wrong with ya if you didn't find that little fox sexy as hell like the rest of us."

Shaking his head in disgust, Jeremiah turned and walked back to his cot. "Naw, just prefer blondes." A lie. He preferred a dark-haired beauty with deep brown eyes and full, pouty lips, but they didn't need to know that.

"Not me," the little punk, Jimmy Wilson, said with a wide grin. "I love the redheads. They like to fight ya. Turns me the fuck on." He'd been working for the General for just over a year now, and Jeremiah hated the prick just as much as the first day he met him, if not more. He was a vile bastard who made it his mission to make all of the prisoners' lives miserable, both male and female. He wanted to beat the hell out of all of the men and have sex with the women. He didn't get to the female prisoners; the General wouldn't have allowed it because he lacked any special psychic abilities. However, the males were a different story. Neither the General, nor anyone working for him, gave a shit who roughed them up. It made Jeremiah sick. He never personally laid a hand on them, but the others didn't realize it. He took great care in making sure it looked as if he was a part of everything that went on. He didn't have a choice. If they found out how deep undercover he was, so deep he'd even cut himself off from his FBI handler, he would be stuck in a cage and on the other side of those fists.

Jeremiah ignored him, glancing at his watch. "My shift starts soon. I'm gonna take a walk first." It was either that or knock the fucker out. Knowing he couldn't get by with that right now, Jeremiah strode from the room, calling back, "Meet ya up front in fifteen, Kyle." He was working with Jerret that night, which was a good thing. He'd probably kill Jimmy if he had to be around him much longer.

Shoving a hand through his thick, brown hair, Jeremiah let his thoughts turn back to the one person in this world that he cared about right now. His mate. Rikki. He felt his fangs punch through his gums at the thought of his woman lying in a hospital bed, oblivious to what was going on around her. He wanted to be with her, not getting ready to patrol the grounds of the facility he was currently stationed in. The General was dead. What the hell was he still doing there? But even as he asked himself the question, Jeremiah knew the answer. The General's death didn't mean the end to the chaos his organization caused. With his daughter, Ebony, taking over, it actually caused a lot more issues than in the beginning. She was more evil than her father, if that were possible. He was going to have a bigger war on his hands than he'd anticipated. One he couldn't fight sitting at his mate's side in the hospital, even if everything in him was telling him that was where he should be right now.

A low growl left his throat, but he forced his fangs to recede, reining in his emotions. He had a mission to accomplish. He needed to focus. Everything he was doing was for Rikki. She was his, and he would do whatever it took to protect her, even if it meant he had to be away from her a little while longer.

Gritting his teeth, Jeremiah nodded to one of the scientists he passed in the hall. Yes, he would bide his time... for now.

3

Rikki woke to the sound of hushed voices in the room, but she lay in silence for a moment with her eyes closed, listening as she tried to acclimate herself to everything going on around her. The sounds and smells in the room were nearly overwhelming, but she fought to stay calm. Breathing deeply in long, slow breaths, she blocked everything out as she forced her racing pulse to slow. She felt a presence in her mind, but refused to panic. She'd felt it before, the last time she woke, and knew what it was, even if she was having a hard time admitting it to herself. There was what felt like a light brush of fur, and then the presence slowly seemed to slip back as if waiting for something.

"Oh! She's awake."

The quiet voice interrupted her thoughts, and Rikki stiffened, her brow furrowing in concentration. She knew that voice. It was familiar to her, even though it didn't belong to one of the members of her team. It wasn't Jenna or Jade. The voice was soft, sweet, always full of joy and excitement. Except when she was talking about the General. Then, she was quiet and the fear crept in. Her body trembled as she remembered the low tone, coated in terror as she talked about him. A low growl filled the room, and Rikki was shocked to discover it was coming from her.

"Rikki, you need to calm down."

She recognized Chase's stern tone, but couldn't seem to stop. She couldn't let go of the protective instincts that had risen with the sweet voice, the need to go after the bastard who had hurt the woman rising in her.

"Hey, little sister. We're here. You're safe."

The words reached her, shoving past the intense feeling of anger that consumed her, and she breathed in deeply, inhaling his scent. Phoenix. Her brother. One of the few people in the world that she trusted. But he didn't seem to understand. She wasn't worried about her safety.

Her eyes springing open, Rikki gazed wildly around the room until her eyes connected with Phoenix's. "Safe. Must keep her safe," she gasped, struggling into a sitting position.

"Who?" Phoenix asked in confusion.

"Can't let the General hurt her again."

"You mean Serenity?" Phoenix slipped his arm around the waist of the beautiful woman standing next to him, her eyes filled with concern as she stared at Rikki. "She and the baby are fine. No one is going to get to them," he promised, his eyes hard as steel.

Rikki's gaze connected with Serenity's, and then her eyes lowered to where Serenity's hand sat protectively over the large mound of her stomach. She gasped, her eyes widening in surprise. Not only was Phoenix's mate pregnant, but she looked as if she was about to give birth any day now.

"I…" Rikki paused. What was she supposed to say? She was… lost. She knew Serenity was pregnant, but how was she suddenly so far along? "I'm so confused."

"Of course, you are. You've been asleep for a long time."

There! That was the voice she was looking for. Rikki's gaze swung to the woman, and the growl came again, this time from deep within her chest. *She* was the one that needed protection. She'd been hurt, tortured by the General's men. Held captive and experimented on for so long. Rikki frowned, her eyes trailing over the stranger. Long blonde hair mixed with red. Amber eyes. Petite frame. She looked unfamiliar, but she wasn't. Rikki knew her. Knew so much about her. How?

"Raven." The name left her lips, and she struggled to slide her legs over the side of the bed. What the hell was wrong with her? Her movements were sluggish when she needed to be on guard. She had to protect her friend.

Rikki heard the gasp of surprise, but ignored it. She had to get the hell out of bed. Raven needed her.

"You know my name?"

Frowning, Rikki paused and looked over at the woman. It took a moment for the shock on Raven's face to register, and then another for her to realize she had somehow sprouted damn claws again. And… were those fangs? Touching the tip of her tongue to her suddenly large incisors, Rikki froze.

"Rikki, it's good to see you are finally back with the land of the living." Doc Josie strode into the room, flashing them a distracted smile as she came to a stop by the bed. "How are you feeling? And why are you trying to get out of bed?"

When the doctor raised an eyebrow and seemed to be waiting for an answer, Rikki's gaze went back to Raven. "Have to protect her from the General," she tried to explain, unsure why she had such a powerful urge to guard the woman. Hell, she didn't even know her, did she?

"Me?" Raven whispered, taking a step toward her, her eyes sparkling with unshed tears. "You want to protect me?"

"He can't have you back," Rikki insisted, once again attempting to rise.

"You're right," Chase cut in, appearing at her side, gently cupping her shoulders and settling her back down on her pillows. "But that's nothing you need to worry about, little wolf. The General is dead. He won't be coming for her."

"What?" Looking over at Raven, Rikki weakly held a hand out to her. "He's gone? You're sure?"

Raven smiled through her tears, quickly crossing the room to slide her hand in Rikki's. "Yes, he's dead. My mate killed him."

"Your mate?" Damn, she was so confused. So tired. By the sounds of it, all she'd been doing lately was sleeping, so why was she utterly exhausted?

"Jaxson."

Rikki's brow furrowed as she fought to recall every-thing she seemed to be forgetting. "I'm tired," she finally whispered, holding tightly to Raven's hand as her eyes went to the doctor. "Why am I so tired?"

"You've been through a lot, Rikki," Doc Josie explained

quietly as she placed a stethoscope to her chest to listen. "It's to be expected. You just need some rest."

"Sounds like I've done enough sleeping," Rikki rasped, letting her head fall back against the pillows. "I want to get up. Move around."

"You know as well as I do that you will fall flat on your face if you get out of that bed," the doctor said, chuckling as she moved the stethoscope around. "Just give it some time. With a little physical therapy and a couple of times shifting, you will be good as new."

"Shifting?" Rikki squeaked, looking at her in horror. What the hell was Josie talking about? She couldn't shift... could she? Refusing to acknowledge the way her teeth and nails had already grown, Rikki shook her head. The part of her that was still human — had always been human — couldn't wrap her mind around the idea of changing into an animal. Even if she had seen many others shift in the past. "I'm not ready for anything like that."

"Well, you better get ready, because your wolf isn't going to wait much longer."

Rikki closed her eyes, struggling to understand everything that was happening. She heard the light rumble from the presence in the back of her mind, knew it was her wolf, but shut her out. She couldn't handle anything else right now.

A light touch settled on her head, and then stroked gently down her head. "Let her rest a little while longer," Raven told them. "She just needs a little time."

"I don't think she has much more time, dragoness. Her wolf is ready to make an appearance."

Dragoness? Rikki raised her eyelids, looking at Raven through mere slits. No fucking way. "You're a dragon?"

she breathed, her hand tightening on the other woman's. "They exist?"

A soft smile covered Raven's lips, and she nodded. "Yes, I am; and they do."

"I had no idea." She wanted to stay awake. Wanted to talk more about this new phenomenon, but couldn't seem to make her eyes stay open. "Raven…"

"I'm right here," Raven replied, sitting down on the bed next to her, holding one hand as she stroked her hair with the other.

"Don't leave."

"I won't," Raven promised.

Rikki let her eyes drift shut again, snuggling deeper into the covers. She heard the conversation going on around her, but it was as if she were listening from a distance. She couldn't respond, couldn't interact, could only listen.

"Why has she latched onto Raven the way she has?" Phoenix questioned. "She doesn't know her. Has never even met her."

"That's incorrect, Phoenix," Doc Josie said quietly. "She may not have ever actually met Raven before, but she knows her very well. You forget, Raven spends more time with her right now than anyone else. She comes here once, sometimes twice a day, and sits for hours talking to her. It doesn't matter that they haven't actually met in person, Rikki knows everything she's heard about her. She remembers."

That made sense, Rikki thought, feeling herself drift a little more. She did know the woman's voice. Knew so many things about her. Where she was from, that she had a brother named Dax, and a sister, Rubi. And, now that she thought about it, she had also known Raven was a dragon. The thought had just slipped her mind before. She even knew about the dragon king, even though, according to Raven, not many people outside of their own kind knew he existed.

"You have become sort of a guideline to her, Raven. Keeping her centered here."

"No," Rikki whispered, shaking her head slowly, surprised she'd managed to get the word out.

"What?"

"Friend," Rikki murmured.

"Ah," Doc Josie said in comprehension. "She is telling me that I am wrong. She considers you her friend, not just someone holding her to us."

"Oh!" She heard the surprise in Raven's voice, and then the pleasure as she went on, "I'm glad. Jaxson has told me so much about her. I want to be her friend, and I'm honored she considers me one."

"She's going to need a lot of help in her recovery process," the doctor said softly. "She needs her friends and family close."

"We'll be here," Phoenix said gruffly. "She's ours. There isn't anything we wouldn't do for her."

Rikki felt herself drifting away again until she heard, "She needs her mate."

"Jeremiah is in the middle of a mission right now."

Her mate. Jeremiah. Her wolf stirred in her mind, and Rikki struggled to open her eyes. What did they mean he was on a mission? Jeremiah didn't go on missions. He had been with the FBI for several years now, and was far enough up in the chain of command that he sent people out on missions but didn't participate in them himself. That's what she did, not him.

"You need to contact him and get his ass home," Josie ordered.

"We can't," Chase said quietly. "He's worked himself so deep undercover, we don't know how to find him."

"Not only that, but what he is doing, he's doing for Rikki. He won't come back until his mission is complete," Phoenix muttered.

What the hell were they talking about? Where was Jeremiah?

"That is unacceptable," the doctor growled, and Rikki swore she heard a foot stomp. "You get that damn bear back here, now!"

Rikki fully agreed, but no matter how hard she tried, she couldn't seem to force her eyes to open, or the words through her lips. She felt a tear slip free and slide down her cheek, then that gentle hand was back on her hair. "It's okay, Rikki. Sshhh, it's all going to be all right. Your mate will be home before you know it, and until then, we will be here for you."

Jeremiah! She needed to find him. Where was he? Was he safe? He better be, or all hell was going to break loose when she got to him. His name was a soft breath on her lips as she finally succumbed to the darkness that had been threatening to overtake her for a while now, terrified that she may not wake up again. Jeremiah!

4

E bony stood looking out the window of the high-rise suite she was staying in for the next couple of days. She was finally free. Free of her father, free to make her own decisions, free to do whatever the hell she wanted, to a certain extent. It had taken her five years of careful planning to put everything into effect. She'd been the General's puppet all of her life, or so he'd thought. In that time, he had molded her into a version of himself; cold, hard, manipulative. Unfortunately, for him, she'd not only excelled, but had become so much more. Her ambition to be the one calling the shots led her to where she was today. Standing in nothing but a short, silky black teddy in front of a row of floor to ceiling windows in the penthouse apartment of one of the leading men in the organization the General had worked for. Some may think she had slept her way to the top. She'd done way more than that. There was so much death and destruction on her hands that she had trouble looking in the mirror sometimes, but it was a price she was willing to pay to be in the position she now held.

"Come back to bed, my darling."

The deep, gravelly voice grated on her nerves. Gavin Denowsky was a very dangerous man, one even she had hesitated in messing with at first, but she'd needed a way in, and he was it. The youngest person on the list of people in the top tier of the organization at fifty-one, Gavin was also single, and male. He was also someone who wouldn't think twice about slitting your throat in your sleep if he thought you were even remotely deserving of it. She treaded very lightly around him, but still used everything available to her advantage.

Turning from the amazing view, Ebony glided across the room in his direction, her gaze raking over his naked body. The man definitely had a superb physique for his age, one she didn't mind playing with in the slightest. Reaching him, she trailed her fingertips lightly over his chest, then down over his stomach, and lower to grasp his already straining cock. Her lips turning up into a sensual grin, she purred, "We don't need a bed for what I have in mind."

His pale blue eyes darkened in desire, and he shoved a hand in the dark strands of her hair, cupping the back of her head and guiding her mouth to his. He wasn't gentle, which was fine with her. She didn't do sweet or slow. She liked it fast, hard, and sometimes with a bite of pain. Ebony moaned as their tongues tangled, and she began to pump his cock. Gavin groaned, his hands sliding under the negligée and yanking it up over her head. Finding her breasts, he tweaked the nipples roughly before ducking his head and capturing one in his mouth, biting down on the end of it.

"Yes!" she cried out, letting go of him to clutch at his shoulders. Moving in closer, she rubbed her aching clit against his thigh, knowing he would take that as the invitation it was.

With a grunt, Gavin cupped her ass in both hands, lifting her up and turning so her back was against the wall. A feral grin crossed his lips as he found her wet entrance with the tip of his cock and pushed deep inside her. "I love fucking you," he muttered, his hands tight on the curve of her ass as he began to pound into her.

"Me, too!" she gasped, throwing her head back as she let a few of the small moans slip free that she knew he liked to hear. Her fingernails dug deep into his shoulders, leaving marks she knew he would look at in satisfaction later. Everything she did was to heighten his desire, get him lost more and more in her, blocking out everything else. She knew what he liked, and she exploited it for all it was worth.

Ebony waited until she was sure he was so lost in pleasure that he wouldn't notice, and then she tentatively reached out psychically, slowly slipping past the protection barriers he had in place, and lightly touched his mind. She had to be very careful, because she had learned quickly that Gavin possessed some strong psychic gifts of his own. She didn't know everything the man was capable of, but she knew enough that she had to have a very light touch because he was powerful. But then, so was she.

Normally, Ebony preferred not to go searching too deeply in someone's mind. Some of them had some really fucked up shit going on. She may be a bitch working her way up the chain of command using almost any means necessary, but even she had her limits. She wanted nothing to do with some of the vile, sick thoughts and feelings some of them had. Unfortunately, it was the only way to get the information she wanted this time. Gavin refused to talk business with her, keeping everything that went on between him and his three business partners confidential, or so he thought. He had no idea she slipped inside his head, taking bits and pieces of his thoughts and memories with her when she left.

Ebony had to push past his sick fantasies, ones that included a couple of women she didn't know chained to a wall, blood dripping down their backs from the slashes of a whip. Another of a woman lying on a bed, tied to the posts, her hungry eyes watching as he slapped a belt into the palm of his hand. She knew he was part of an underground club that liked things even rougher than she did. She refused to play those games with him. She would never allow anyone to bind her in anyway. It would give them too much power. Now, if he wanted her to tie him up, she was all for that.

"Fuck," Gavin snarled, burying his face in her neck. She felt his teeth latch on to her skin, but didn't try to stop him. Gavin was human, but for some reason, he had a fetish for biting during sex. She didn't care. Whatever kept him distracted while she delved inside his brain.

Letting her breathing become more labored, her chest heaving, she raked her hands down his back, her nails digging deep the way he liked it. It drove him wild, and his hips began to piston even faster. When she was positive he was too distracted with what was going on with his lower head to worry about the upper one, she dug deep, extracting whatever information she could. What she found had her smiling, and she decided to give him something extra for the information he had no idea he shared with her. Leaning down, she bit deep into the skin on his shoulder, smiling in satisfaction when he roared her name before coming deep inside of her. Soon, she was following him over the edge.

Moments later, Ebony let her legs fall from his hips, and Gavin lowered her to the floor. When he raised his head to look at her, a thin layer of sweat covering his brow, she grinned. "How about a quick shower before I go?'

"Where are you going?" he demanded, frowning slightly. "You said you had a couple of days this time."

"I do," she agreed. Sauntering toward the kitchen, she turned back with a sultry smile. "I have a bit of work I need to do tonight. Then, I'll be back. But first, I need a drink and another quick fuck in the shower." She had a ferocious sexual appetite, and it would take more than what they had just shared to sate her. Luckily, he was the same, and her words had his dick plumping again.

"I'll get the water started."

"I'll bring the wine," she purred.

JINX WAITED IMPATIENTLY for Ebony to arrive, the thought of answering to her now instead of the General leaving him in a constant state of pissed the fuck off. He was angry with himself for underestimating the conniving bitch, mad as hell that he hadn't moved fast enough to protect the General, even if he had hated the bastard, and wondering if he should just walk away from it all. The problem was, he couldn't for several reasons. The main one being he had no idea where Ebony stashed Amber, and he needed that information before he did anything else. Amber was innocent in everything that was going on. Her biggest sin was helping the shifters who were being held and tortured by her father. Because of that, because she actually gave a damn about others, her sister sentenced her to living the life the prisoners they held were forced to live. He had managed to get that much out of Ebony. She'd bragged about it, letting him know he would have to find a piece of ass somewhere else now if he had been interested in her sister. He wouldn't want her when they were done with her. Jinx wasn't interested in Amber, not for himself. She belonged to his uncle. She was mate to his dad's brother, Bane, and shit was going to hit the fan really quick if he couldn't find her. Not only that, but she was kind, caring, sweet. She didn't deserve what she was being put through.

Jinx knew Ebony was there before he saw her. He felt her presence; evil to the core. He glared at her as she walked toward him, knowing his eyes were glowing that odd green they did when he was angry. He didn't care. Let her see he was pissed. She'd kept him waiting for over two hours, while it looked, and smelled, as if she was out getting laid.

"Jinx," she said, a slow smile crossing her lips as she let her gaze wander over him. "Been here long?"

"Why did you call me, Ebony?" he asked in a bored tone, refusing to let her goad him into a response he knew he would regret. She was, after all, his boss now.

"I thought you might be interested in getting to know

me a little better," she murmured, stepping in close to him and resting a hand lightly on his chest.

Jinx inhaled deeply, cocking an eyebrow. "I think you've already had enough of that tonight."

Ebony's lips turned up in a pout and she shrugged. "Maybe, but he wasn't you."

No, he wasn't, thank fuck. Jinx had no desire to have his dick anywhere near the piranha. "What do you want, Ebony?"

Her dark eyes narrowed, and she glared at him as she fisted his shirt. "Don't forget who you answer to now, dog."

"Dog?" he laughed, barely resisting the urge to shove her from him. "Is that the best you got?"

Ebony's facial expression turned hard, a muscle ticking in her jaw, her lips firming. Her hand tightened on his shirt, pulling him closer. "I'm going to let this go for now, Jinx, but trust me, you do not want to push me."

"Or else what?" he drawled, stiffening when she moved until their bodies were touching.

"Or else, I will kill everyone you love," she vowed, her eyes glittering with malice.

"I'm a coldhearted assassin, remember? I don't feel love."

"So, it wouldn't bother you at all if I went after your sister, then?"

"I don't know," he muttered, baring his teeth at her. "Why don't you try it and see?" He would tear her heart out if she came near any of his sisters: Jade, Faith, or Hope. Right at that moment, he was hoping she would make the mistake of trying.

Ebony stared at him in silence for a full minute before

throwing her head back and laughing. Smoothing her hand down his chest, she shrugged and took a step back. "I don't care about your sister at this time, or anyone else. What I do care about, is power."

No shit. "Go on."

"I've been spending my time with someone special lately, Jinx. Someone you would be very interested in."

"I doubt it."

Arching an eyebrow, she asked, "What would you say if I told you I've got an in with the people the General answered to?" When he didn't respond, she went on, "Not just the ones right above him in the food chain, but the ones at the very top."

Jinx froze, his eyes narrowing as he watched Ebony closely. Was she lying? If she was, she was very good, because he couldn't scent it. "I'm listening."

Crossing her arms over her chest, Ebony said, "There are four of them on the board. That's what they call it. They are in charge of all decision making in the organization. You don't take a piss without them knowing."

Jinx called bullshit on that one. He did a lot of things no one else knew about. "Go on."

"There are three men, and one woman. Gavin Denowsky, Hamilton Reed, Dayton Burns, and Victoria Smelt. They have equal say in all matters, but there is a power struggle going on."

"Which one are you sleeping with?" It was a guess, but he knew it was accurate. She'd somehow crawled her way into the circle of four, and was now monitoring them even though they had no clue. It was one of her specialties, getting inside someone's head and finding out all of their secrets. She told him once that she hated it, and he'd been surprised to find she was telling the truth, but it never stopped her from using the skill.

"Gavin," she replied with a shrug. "He's the youngest."

"And single," he guessed.

"Exactly." Jinx watched her gaze skate around the area before she went on, "He was also the easiest to get to. I had nothing at all in common with the others. Gavin and I have one thing in common."

"Sex."

"Correct."

"How did you figure out who he and the others were?" Hell, he'd been trying for months to find out who the head of the organization was without any leads. She was already in bed with one of them.

"I followed the General to a meeting he had with one of his superiors once," she explained. "Then, I followed them and so on until I eventually got to where I needed to be."

"What's your end game?"

"What is it always, Jinx?" she asked, resting her hands lightly on her hips. "Power. I want more of it."

He paused, watching her closely, then guessed, "You want a place on the board."

"Yes."

"Why are you telling me all of this?"

"Because, you are going to help me make that happen," Ebony said, "and in return, you will be rewarded."

"How?" What could she possibly have that he wanted?

"You leave that to me. Just know, it will definitely be worth it."

5

R ikki wiped the sweat from her brow before grasping the walker tightly and taking another step. After her long ass nap — around five months from what she'd been told — she was having an issue getting her body to work the way it was supposed to. Doc Josie tried numerous times to get her to shift, telling her it would go a long way in helping her recover, but she was terrified to let this new side of her out. She could feel the power of her wolf. It was like nothing Rikki had ever felt before, and she was afraid she wouldn't be able to control her once she was free. She didn't want anyone to get hurt, and with all of the turbulent emotions pouring through her right now, it was a very real possibility that someone could.

It had been two days since she heard Phoenix talking about Jeremiah, but no one would tell her anything. They refused, saying it would be best if she waited for Angel. Even Chase kept quiet. For some reason, her wolf was having difficulties accepting him as her alpha. And, if she were honest, she was, too. The only alpha she wanted was Angel.

Rikki grew up in various foster homes until she ran away at the age of fifteen and began living on the streets. It was a tough life, but with her special ability of being able to touch an object and see the past, present, and sometimes the future, living around people was hard. She'd learned to adapt, and it was easier on the streets, following her own rules and staying away from others. At the age of eighteen, she decided she was strong enough, disciplined enough, to leave the streets and venture out into the world. She decided to enlist in the army, and ended up serving two terms, becoming one of the best snipers they'd ever had. Once she left the military, she'd been lost for a few months. Then, she met Angel. The woman offered her a chance to save lives using the skills she'd been trained for in the army, but never thought she would put them into play again. She found a family the day she accepted Angel's offer — the first family she ever had — and she would do anything for them.

Grunting in frustration, Rikki moved the walker faster down the hall. She felt the need to fight, to push harder and harder, until she was the person she used to be before one of the General's men put a bullet in her. Something bad was about to happen, she could feel it. Her mate needed her. As that thought slipped into Rikki's head, she felt the brush of fur against her mind. Claws sprang from her fingertips and fangs punched through her gums. She was getting used to it. It seemed to happen anytime she was upset or angry, or just plain over emotional, and her wolf sensed she needed her. Which was a lot. This time was different, though. She tried to shove the bitch back down. Struggled to make her claws recede. It wasn't happening. It was as if she had no control over her own body.

"Rikki?" The voice was soft, hesitant. Jade.

Rikki swung around, baring her teeth at the young woman. "Get back," she growled, afraid she wasn't going to be able to get control back from her wolf. Jade was her friend, and she didn't want to hurt her.

"Rikki, it's going to be okay," Jade rushed to reassure her. "Your wolf won't harm you. She only wants to help."

"It's not me I'm worried about," Rikki admitted through clenched teeth. Her fangs bit into her lips and she snarled, her eyes pleading with her friend. "Please, Jade, back away. I can't stop her this time."

"You don't need to," a warm voice full of understanding said, and Rikki's gaze swung around to see Angel striding down the long hall toward her. "It's okay, Rikki. I'm so sorry I wasn't here when you woke up, but I'm here now."

"I can't stop it, Angel," Rikki rasped, letting go of the walker and dropping to her knees. Pain slammed up her spine, and Rikki arched her back, a scream tearing from her throat. "Angel!"

She felt a hand on her shoulder and flinched away in pain and confusion.

"Rikki, trust me. It's going to be all right. Feel your wolf. Let her presence flow through you," Angel murmured, stroking a long strand of dark hair away from her face.

"She's so strong," Rikki gasped, a hard shudder racking her body. "What if she hurts somebody?"

"She won't," Angel promised, gently running a hand down her back. "All she wants to do is help you, Rikki. Shifting will make you stronger. You will be good as new after a couple of times."

"She wants Jeremiah," Rikki corrected, throwing her head back and baring her teeth when another sharp slice of agony raced up her spine. It felt as if her body was contorting in on itself. Bones were popping, muscles contracting. "She senses he's in danger. Wants to get to him."

"Jeremiah is fine," Angel promised. "I just saw him a few weeks ago. He looks good, and is stubborn as hell, just like always."

Rikki's mouth twisted in agony as she spat, "Not true! He's not fine! He's with the General."

"The General is dead."

Rikki glared at Angel, snarling, "With his fucking daughter, then. I'm going to find her, Angel. I'm going to fucking kill her."

Angel's light blue gaze darkened, and she leaned in to rub her cheek against Rikki's. Rikki sighed at the contact, and at the subtle feel of power radiating from her alpha. Her true alpha. "Well, you can't do that in the shape you are in right now. So, why don't you shift? Then we can start training in a couple of days and go hunting for your mate once you are back up to speed."

A deep growl rumbled through her, and suddenly her vision changed, seeming to blur at first, and then sharpen. Rikki sucked in a breath when she realized she was seeing through the eyes of her wolf.

"That's it," Angel crooned, pushing some more alpha power toward Rikki. "Let your wolf come out."

"Get everyone back," Rikki snarled around her fangs, shaking in fear and pain. She was drawing a crowd, and she could feel her wolf getting nervous. "I can't let her hurt anyone."

"You need to stop thinking of your wolf as a separate being from you," Chase said, approaching them cautiously. "She's a part of you, Rikki. One and the same. You would never hurt anyone in this hospital, which means neither would she."

"I would if they were a threat to my mate."

"That's no different than anyone else here." Doc Josie's voice was calm, but the woman stayed back, motioning for others to do the same. "I would protect my mate at all cost."

"Me, too," Chase agreed, kneeling down next to them. "I would gut anyone who threatened Angel in my presence. It's in our genetics to protect those we love, especially our mates. They hold the other half of our soul. Without them, we are nothing."

Breathing heavily, panting through the pain, Rikki thought about what they said. She heard the truth in their voices. Didn't smell the acrid scent she had come to associate with a lie over the past couple of days. One of the nurses insisted on telling her she wasn't afraid of her, but Rikki smelled the stench of her lie every single time. The woman did her job, never once giving in to that fear, but it was there.

"It's the truth. I hate fighting, but if anyone threatened my mate, my dragon would roast them all."

Rikki swallowed hard, her gaze rising to meet Raven's.

The dragoness had become a close friend after sharing so much of her life with her, both when Rikki was in her sleeping state, and the past two days when she was wide awake. One she trusted, and she didn't trust easily. Tears filling her eyes, Rikki reached for Raven, needed the reassurance the other woman gave her.

"Raven." Jaxson placed a hand on Raven's arm, looking from her to Rikki in concern.

"I'll be fine." Raven pulled away from him, rushing over to Rikki. Dropping to her knees, she grasped her hand tightly.

"I don't want to hurt you," Rikki rasped, moaning as another wave of pain rolled through her.

"I'm a dragon, my friend," Raven said dryly, leaning in to touch her forehead to Rikki's. "I have bigger claws, longer and sharper fangs. You can't hurt me." Raven let her fangs drop, grinning widely as she showed them to Rikki. "See?"

Rikki's eyes widened as she looked at the huge teeth, a hint of laughter escaping, that quickly turned into a grimace of pain. Gasping, she whispered, "Why does it hurt so much?"

"Because you are fighting it," Angel said quietly. "Let go, Rikki. Let your wolf merge with you. Become one with each other. Trust me."

She did trust Angel, but she was still terrified. No matter how many times she'd seen her team members turn into their animals, the thought of doing it herself was scary as hell.

"I'm right here," Raven said softly, her amber eyes full of sympathy and concern. "We all are. Let your wolf free, Rikki. We will protect both of you, even from yourself."

Rikki glanced down to where their hands were clasped together, seeing Raven's large claws emerge. It was what she needed to hear. Her team was there, and Angel may have been her alpha, but she knew without a doubt that the dragon in front of her could protect not only her, but everyone in the hospital with them if something were to go terribly wrong. Slowly, she took a deep breath and tried to let go.

Once she let her wolf in, allowing the animal to merge with her, the pain immediately started to lessen. It was still there, but it was as if her wolf was shouldering some of it now. Rikki groaned as she felt a change taking over her body. She started to panic when she felt her face transform, her jawline, mouth, and nose elongating into a snout. She forced the shift to stop, her entire body shaking with the effort. A whine slipped free, but Raven, Angel, and Chase were all there instantly.

"Come on, Rikki," Angel growled. "You are stronger than this. Don't let your fears control you. Hit those bastards head on. You got this!"

Raven leaned down and looked her in the eye. "You can do this, my friend. For you, for Jeremiah, for everyone who loves you. Stand strong. Be proud of the person you are becoming, proud of the wolf you now share your life with. She's proud of you."

"She is?" Rikki panted, sweat dripping down her cheeks.

"Yes, I can tell. She's happy she was chosen to be yours. It's time to show her that you feel the same way."

"We are right here," Chase promised, and she could feel him pushing some of his power her way. Whereas before it bothered her, now, with Angel there, it seemed right.

Rikki began to calm, and closing her eyes, she allowed herself to fully connect with the wolf who waited patiently. There was pain and fear, but there was also determination. She could do this. She would do it. For Jeremiah, she could do anything. And if shifting would get her to him that much faster, then there was no other choice. Hell, her wolf wasn't giving her one even if she wanted one.

A low growl rumbled deep in her chest, rising from her throat, and then a loud howl split the air as she shifted. One second, she was kneeling on the ground in a hospital gown with her signature black gloves on her hands that blocked the visions from constantly coming. The next, she was laying on the cold tile on her belly, with four paws, a tail, and covered in fur. She panted heavily as her gaze swept the area around her, too tired and weak to rise to her feet. The anger that she was afraid of was still there, but it was tempered by the love she felt for those who were close to her. She had been so scared the rage that was bottled up inside would come out and she would hurt one of them, but she had nothing to worry about. The wolf wasn't angry at them. She had no desire to tear their throats out. She was saving it all for the General's daughter and men. They were the ones she wanted to take her aggression out on. They were the ones who were going to pay.

Rikki stiffened at first when she felt a soothing hand trail over her back, but somehow she knew it was Angel, and she slowly let herself accept the touch, laying her head down on her paws. Raven stroked the fur on her neck gently, smiling. "There. See, that wasn't so bad, was it?"

Rikki was too exhausted to respond. She knew she would be able to talk to them telepathically in the form she was in, but she just didn't have the energy. She was just too damn tired to do anything.

"Rest, little wolf," Chase said gruffly, sliding his arms under her and lifting her in the air. When she started to struggle sluggishly, he pulled her close. "I'm just taking you back to your room."

She was vaguely aware of Angel walking beside them, and Raven picking up her gown and gloves and following them down the hall, Jaxson right behind her. Nico was there, too, and Trace. Her team. Chase laid her gently on her bed, rubbing a hand across her fur before saying, "You are beautiful, Rikki. Your coat is a stunning brown and black mixture, with some white in there, too."

"It's just gorgeous," Angel murmured, squatting down so Rikki could look at her without raising her head. "I am so proud of you, Rikki. I know it took a lot of courage to finally accept your wolf. It won't always be easy, but I can promise you that she will always be a part of you. She will always want to protect you. Trust in her, and she will trust in you."

Rikki tried to nod, but wasn't sure if it worked or not. She was vaguely aware of Phoenix's voice outside her room, loudly demanding to know what the hell was going on. Chase and Angel walked away from the bed to talk quietly by the window, but Raven didn't leave her. She set Rikki's gloves on the table beside the bed, and then climbed up beside her. Lying down on her side, she gently ran her hand over Rikki's back before whispering, "Get some sleep now, Rikki. I'll be right here when you wake up. I promise."

Rikki had no idea how the other woman knew she needed to hear that, needed someone nearby when her emotions were in so much turmoil, but she was glad Raven was staying with her. Closing her eyes, she snuggled up close to her friend and slowly let herself drift off to sleep.

6

"You're being transferred to the Virginia facility."

The news didn't surprise him. They never kept the guards in the same place for too long. He had been at eight different facilities in the months he'd been working for the General. Never in one place long enough to become attached to anyone or anything. At least, he assumed that was the reason they switched the guards around so often. However, this was the first time they were sending him back to one he'd already been to.

"When?"

"Effective immediately," was the response.

"I'll get my things."

"You will be going alone this time. We are sending Kyle to a different place."

That did surprise him. Jerret Kyle had been his tagalong since he started, which could only mean one thing. He'd finally earned their trust. He was in. "Got it. I'll leave within the hour."

Standing, Jeremiah resisted the urge to send the bastard behind the desk a mock salute. Dan Masters was in charge of the place he was currently stationed at in Phoenix, Arizona. Masters had been in the military for over thirty years, and ran the facility with an iron hand. He was efficient, loyal to the cause, and a complete dickhead. Just like most of the men under Ebony's command. Damn, that took some getting used to. Ebony, not the General anymore. He still couldn't believe the asshole was dead. A part of him was thrilled. The part that loved his mate and wanted nothing more than the asshole to be gone after everything he'd done to Rikki.

Another part, the part that was ruled by his bear, was jealous because he was the one who'd wanted to tear out the General's throat. But a bigger part of him, the man who had worked for the FBI for several years and had been around shit like this for so long it made his gut ache just thinking about it, knew there was going to be hell to pay after what happened. While the General may have been referred to as the devil in the past, Satan's daughter was way worse than he ever was. She had her eye on the prize — as much power as she could hope to get — and was plowing her way to the top. She didn't care who she hurt, or killed, in the process. There was going to be a lot of death and destruction in the future, even more than would have been caused by the General. Of that, Jeremiah had no doubt.

"Check in with Lenox Keaton as soon as you get there. He is expecting you sometime in the next couple of days."

Jeremiah frowned in confusion. "I'm not flying out right away?"

"No, we need you to take one of the Hummers. They are down a couple of vehicles and need it to transport a prisoner somewhere."

That didn't make sense at all. Why the hell would they want him to take a Hummer when there were other facilities closer that would have them? "I don't understand."

"It isn't your job to question the decisions of those above you," Masters snarled. "Get your things and meet up with Kyle. You will be dropping him off in New Mexico on the way."

"Yes, sir."

"Jeremiah."

"Yeah?"

"Don't fuck this up."

Jeremiah raised an eyebrow. Don't fuck what up? What the hell was he getting at? What was there to fuck up? Shaking his head, Jeremiah turned and left the room after a muttered, "Yes, sir."

Stalking down the hall, he quickly made his way to the room he shared with the other guards. Jerret was already there, throwing his things in a bag. Glancing up when Jeremiah entered, he grinned, "Looks like we are moving on. Just as well. This place is fucking boring compared to others I've been at."

Which meant there weren't as many prisoners to screw with. There were only two there at the time, both males. The lion, Cian, and a wolf who refused to give his name to anyone. Jeremiah didn't blame him. Giving someone your name gave them power. He'd debated on using an alias when he first began to infiltrate the General's ranks for that reason, but decided to keep his first name. It was easier than learning a new one, and he couldn't afford any mistakes when it came to this mission. He did change his surname to Jenson. It was common and unobtrusive.

"Yeah. Sounds like I'm taking you to New Mexico. Never been there before."

"Me neither. Hope it's better than this one."

Jeremiah grabbed his bag and shoved his guard uniforms into it. After packing his things from the bathroom, he picked up two books off the dresser.

"I don't understand why you like to read that shit," Kyle said, zipping up his duffle bag. "Hell, we live it. Why do you want to read it, too?"

Jeremiah glanced down at the thriller novels in his hand, then shrugged as he tossed them into his bag. Closing it, he grasped the handles and grinned. "It's exciting."

"Death turns you on?"

"It doesn't you?" Jeremiah asked, raising an eyebrow. Yeah, death turned him on, as long as it was the death of a cold-hearted bastard like the one standing in front of him.

An evil smirk crossed Kyle's face. "Hell yeah, it does."

Shaking his head, Jeremiah let his grin linger, even though he wanted nothing more than to punch his claws through Kyle's chest and show him how much he would like someone's death right now. "Reading is good for the soul. Maybe you should try it sometime."

"Screw that. I have other things I would much rather be doing that are a lot better for my soul." Grabbing his bag, he stalked toward the door. "Let's go. I'm ready for a change. Hopefully, New Mexico will give me that."

Jeremiah followed him to the parking garage, his duffle bag slung over his shoulder. He was ready for a change, too. But not for anything Virginia had to offer. No, everything he wanted, that he craved, was in Colorado. Which was just north of New Mexico. They were giving him two days to get to Virginia. Would that give him enough time to sneak up to Colorado and check on his mate? It would be tight, but if he dropped Kyle off and then drove hellbent, he could do it. He would only have a couple of hours to see Rikki, but that was all he needed. Something in him was pushing him to Colorado. To his mate. He needed to make sure she was all right.

He and Kyle threw their bags in the back of the Hummer, and then climbed in the front, Jeremiah behind the wheel. Yeah, it would be tight, and there was every chance he wouldn't make it to Virginia in time, but that wasn't going to stop him. The pull to see his mate was strong. Stronger than anything else at the moment. Just to lay eyes on her. Make sure she was breathing. That was all he needed, all his bear needed. Then, he would jump back into hell. The driving need was something he couldn't ignore.

Pulling out of the garage, he carefully made his way over the rough terrain until he hit the highway. He ran ten miles per hour over the speed limit until he hit New Mexico. After dropping Jerret off, he left, heading toward Virginia. When he was sure he wasn't being followed, he pulled the vehicle over at a gas station. After a quick once-over, he began to look more closely at the Hummer's undercarriage, until he found the tracker. Removing it, he very carefully dismantled it, just enough that it would look as if it were a technical malfunction, before reattaching it. When he was satisfied, he filled the tank with gas and then climbed back in. Soon, he was on the road headed toward the White River Wolves compound going ninety-five.

7

Rikki stood facing Storm, chest heaving as she growled, "Why are you holding back on me?"

"Rikki, you just got out of the hospital three days ago. You are still recovering after everything you've been through. I don't want to hurt you."

"That's not going to happen," Rikki snarled. "All you are doing right now is pissing me off. I've shifted twice since that first time. I'm moving around just fine. I'm running, lifting weights. I feel good. Like my normal self. Let's do this!"

"Rikki," Storm seemed to hesitate as she glanced over to where Angel and Steele stood watching them. "You may feel fine, but you haven't sparred in months. There is a chance that I could hurt you, and I don't want to do that."

"Then get someone else in here," Rikki spat, turning to Angel. "I am never going to get stronger and be where I need to be if someone doesn't challenge me, dammit."

"I'll do it," Phoenix growled, walking toward them

from the barn. They were at Angel's farm, where they spent the days working out, sparring, and shooting when they weren't out on a mission. Against many protests, Rikki had been there since she left the hospital, even choosing to stay overnight. She'd already spent several hours at the shooting range and was happy to see that she was up to par there. Now, she just needed to get back to her full strength. She needed to spar.

"Fine. Let's go."

"No holding back?" he asked, motioning Storm away as he stopped in front of Rikki. "Cause, I'm gonna put you on your ass, little sister. Over and over again. You've had a fucking attitude ever since you opened those pretty brown eyes of yours, and I'm getting sick and tired of it."

"I do not," she protested, clenching her hands into fists, her nails digging into her skin.

"You've been snapping and snarling at everyone," he growled. "Why is that?'

"I'm not."

"Yes," he snarled, "you are. And you know it."

Rikki began to shake, rage pouring through her. "Fuck off, Phoenix."

Phoenix began to walk slowly in a circle around her, shuffling his feet to the right. "It's the truth. Every member of this team came to see you at the hospital, even the ones you hadn't met yet. We all tried to get you to talk to us, but you wouldn't. We can feel your anger, Rikki, but we don't know why. Do you have any idea what we've been going through these past few months? How much we've all missed you? We were scared to death that you wouldn't wake up. That you would choose to move on instead of coming back to us. And then, when you finally do wake up to face the world, you treat us like crap. We're family."

Rikki felt her claws lengthen, and she bared her teeth at him in anger. "What *you've* gone through? What about me, Phoenix? What about what I went through?" Pissed off, she lunged in, slicing her claws over his arm before leaping back out of his way. She forced her claws to retract, knowing it would be hard to throw a punch with them. And that was what she wanted right now. To pound the shit out of something, or someone. At this point, it didn't matter who it was.

Glancing down at the blood dripping from his wound, Phoenix raised an eyebrow. "Cheap shots aren't like you, Rikki."

"All's fair in love and war," she snapped back, kicking out quickly, her foot connecting with his gut before she quickly spun away on the balls of her feet. A wave of dizziness swamped her, but she pushed it aside. She didn't have time for weakness right now. She had to fight, had to get stronger.

The punch to her side shocked the hell out of her, and her eyes widened when pain shot through her. A small whimper escaped before she could stop it, but she bit her lip, forcing the pain away. Blocking it so she could concentrate.

"Phoenix," Angel said quietly. "Maybe this isn't the right way."

"This is the only way," he growled. "We've given her time, but she's been nothing but a bitch to us. I'm tired of handling her with kid gloves. She wants a fight, she's got it."

"Kid gloves?" Rikki snarled. "I'll show you kid gloves!"

She was on him in seconds, all in. Short, powerful jabs connected with his abs, and then an uppercut to his chin and a fist to the face. Dancing away, she was right back with a sweep of her foot, knocking him on his ass.

Phoenix was up and on his feet before she knew it, throwing an arm up to block her next punch. "So, that's how it is?" he snarled.

"What?" she jeered. "You can't handle a little sparring? I thought you were better than this, Phoenix?"

Shaking his head, Phoenix wiped at the blood dripping down his chin, his eyes flashing to his wolf and back in anger. "What the hell has gotten into you, Rikki?"

"Rikki, whatever is wrong, this is not the way," Angel said in a low tone. "Trust me."

"Trust you?" Rikki growled, turning to her alpha. "I *did* trust you, and look where it got me."

Pain flashed through Angel's eyes, and she moved closer to Chase, leaning into him for support. "I'm sorry, Rikki."

"I trusted *all* of you!" Rikki cried.

"I don't understand," Nico said in confusion, appearing from around the side of the barn. "You know you can trust us, Rikki. We're family."

Target practice must be over, Rikki thought in a huff as more and more of the team showed up. She bared her teeth at them as a low growl rumbled in her chest. Of course, they didn't understand. How could they? Most of them were with their mates every night, while she had no idea where hers was. If it was one of theirs, they wouldn't be standing around here at Angel's farm, they'd be out looking for the ones they loved.

"Rikki..."

Rikki swung around and bared her teeth at Angel when the alpha moved from her mate's embrace and took a step in her direction. "Stay away from me." Rikki glared at them as she slowly turned in a circle. "All of you, stay the hell away from me."

"That's enough," Chase growled, his hand on Angel's arm halting her movement. "I know you are going through a lot right now, little wolf, which is the only reason I'm giving you a free pass this time. You will not disrespect my mate again."

"You are not my alpha," Rikki snarled, her eyes trained on the dangerous man.

"Yes, Rikki, he is," Nico said quietly. "We have all sworn our allegiance to the White River Wolves. Once Chase and Angel fully mated, he became our alpha, and Angel his alpha mate. We answer to both of them."

She knew Angel had finally accepted Chase's mate claim, hadn't thought anything beyond that. Now, Rikki's heart constricted as she realized what that meant. There would be two people who had control over her, not just Angel. It was hard enough for her to answer to Angel, she was afraid having to obey both would be nearly impossible. Her chest tightened, her breath coming in short, harsh pants. "I haven't," she rasped. "I follow Angel, and only Angel."

"That's not the way it works," Angel said, pulling away from Chase to walk over to Rikki. "I am so sorry, my friend. This is all my fault. I just couldn't let you go, but I never thought about what it would mean to you. I know how difficult all of this must be for you, with your past."

Everything was crowding in around her, and her wolf was rising quickly to the surface. Rikki tried to shove her back down, somehow knowing a lot of the issues she was having right now were because of her, but it wasn't working. "I agreed," she whispered, her hands out to her sides as she clenched and unclenched her fingers, her claws punching through the tips of her fingers.

"Yes, but you were in so much agony," Angel said, reaching out to place a gentle hand on her arm. Chase growled deeply in warning, but she ignored him. "You were bleeding out quickly, almost gone from us. You weren't thinking clearly, and neither was I."

Shaking her head, Rikki reiterated, "I agreed."

"Yes, but you didn't fully know what you were agreeing to."

Lifting her head, Rikki met her light blue gaze. "Yes, I did. I wanted to live, Angel. I didn't want to leave this world. I didn't want to leave my mate."

Angel's brow furrowed, and she let her hand fall to her side. "That isn't what this is about? Your anger at being turned?"

"And it can't be about Chase being your alpha, because you didn't understand that until just now," Flame said, her hands resting lightly on her hips. Cocking her head to the side, her long auburn hair resting over the swell of her breasts, she asked, "Does it have something to do with Jeremiah? Cause if I've learned anything this past year living with shifters, it's that the one thing that makes them lose control is if it involves their mates. It would only stand to reason, as angry as you've been, that this has something to do with yours."

Angel gasped, her eyes widening in comprehension. "That's what this is about, isn't it, Rikki? Jeremiah? Why would you be so angry at us about him?"

Rikki's wolf pushed to the surface, and before she knew what was happening, she began to shift.

"Rikki?"

"You didn't save him!" Rikki ground out, past the fangs that had erupted in her mouth.

"Save him?" Angel frowned, shaking her head. "Rikki, I can't help what Jeremiah…"

Before she could finish her sentence, Rikki snarled, "He's my mate! That makes him family! You should have brought him home to me. Instead, you all left him there. With that bitch, Ebony. My mate is in danger, and it's *your* fault. You *left* him!"

Chase quickly closed the distance between them, his finger going into a loop on Angel's pants. Tugging, he hauled her back next to him, away from Rikki who was in mid-shift.

"No!" Angel said, shaking her head in denial. "He left us, Rikki! Once we figured out what he was doing, we searched for him. So many times. No matter how hard we tried, we couldn't find him. He was evading us. This last time, when we saw him, we tried to get him to come home. He wouldn't listen. He walked away from us. There was nothing we could do."

Rikki froze, pain slamming into her at Angel's admission. Her mate had walked away from them? From her? Slowly, her fangs receded, and she collapsed to the ground. He'd had the chance to come home, to be with her, but he'd chosen to walk away? Her heart shattered in her chest, and a loud howl ripped from her throat. Her mate had left her.

"Oh, Rikki," Angel whispered, tearing from her mate's arms and dropping to her knees beside her. Reaching out tentatively, she placed a comforting hand on Rikki's shoulder. "He didn't want to leave you. He loves you so damn much. He's doing what he is doing because of how much he cares. He's trying to get rid of everyone who could cause you harm."

A shudder rippled through her, and Rikki threw back her head and howled in despair again. Maybe he was doing what he was out of love for her, but it didn't change the fact that he could have come home. Instead, he chose to walk away from her. If he really wanted her, wouldn't he be there right now?

"Rikki, listen to me," Phoenix growled, kneeling beside them. "Think about it. That man loves you enough to be out there fighting a war that could get him killed. He's in the middle of the fucking trenches. He's worked himself so far deep into all of it, that if they found out who he is, his death would not be an easy one. But he's doing it for you. Because he loves you." Rikki stiffened, the thought of Jeremiah in that much danger brought her wolf to the surface again. Her gaze locking with Phoenix's, she growled, her eyes flashing wolf and back. He leaned in, placing his forehead to hers. "I say, get mad, little sister. Get pissed the fuck off. Get up and fight. That man doesn't need you laying in the dirt crying. He needs you fighting for him, like he is doing for you."

Slowly, Rikki pulled away from Angel and stood. She was shaking, the struggle against letting her wolf free a hard one. "She's angry," Rikki rasped, closing her eyes and taking a deep breath. "So angry."

"Your wolf?"

Rikki nodded. "She's mad as hell at the world. I'm having a hard time controlling her."

"That's why you are so pissed at everyone," Angel said quietly as she rose to her feet and stepped back by her mate. "Your wolf is."

Her eyes fluttering open, Rikki whispered, "She doesn't understand why he isn't here...and neither do I."

"Because he's a dumbass," Trace muttered.

"She wants out," Rikki admitted, ignoring him. "Wants to fight someone. Something. I try to push her back down, but it's so hard."

"So, let her out," Phoenix said, a small grin turning up the corners of his mouth. "Maybe a good rumble is all she needs."

"What?"

His hands going to the snap on his jean, his grin widened. "It's been a week or so since I've sparred in wolf form. Let's have a little fun."

"Fun?"

"Hey, just don't go for the throat."

Her eyes went to his hands, and her cheeks colored. "Can't you go do that in the barn?" she snapped. "I don't want to see your dick flying around. Jesus, you're like my freaking brother."

Nico let out a roar of laughter. "There's our Rikki."

8

J eremiah managed to not only get inside the White River Wolves compound, but also slip into the hospital unnoticed, with the help of a special pill the General's scientists had developed that masked his scent. He also had one that helped block the ability of psychics to slide inside his mind and another that altered the perception of anyone he gave it to. He avoided using the last one, because he hated the thought of messing with anyone's head. Also, it was still in the testing phase and had really screwed up some of the test subjects, causing them to kill themselves. But the first two pills he used on a regular basis. It was how he managed to stay one step ahead of RARE when they were hunting him earlier in the year.

He found what had to be Rikki's room. Her scent was there, even though it was faint, making his cock immediately stand to attention. Jeremiah groaned under his breath, pushing down on the annoying prick, hoping to ease the discomfort. He didn't have time for a distraction. There was too much at stake right now.

The bed was made, the room clean. Rikki may have been there, but not for a few days. Fear began to fill him at what that might mean. Where the hell was she? Alive, or... he wouldn't let himself continue that thought. His mate was not dead. He would know it. He would feel it deep down inside.

"So, she's okay?"

Jeremiah stiffened at the sound of a female voice right outside the door. Shit. He'd been caught up in his own thoughts, missing the fact that someone was near.

"Well, she should be fine to spar. Just watch her closely. Her wolf is strong, and from what you are saying, she's very angry. You need to be careful who you give her as a target to take her aggression out on. If it is someone she doesn't know very well, she could hurt them. She won't have any reason to pull back."

Jeremiah's eyes narrowed at the conversation. What was going on?

"How long will everyone be at Angel's? I would like you to bring Rikki back here afterwards so I can do another exam. I'm sure she's fine, but it's better to err on the side of caution."

Rikki. She was at Angel's. That was all he needed to know. If she was there, that meant she was fine. Safe.

"I know. That woman is so stubborn. Just try to get her here."

Yes, his Rikki was stubborn as hell, and so damn beautiful his dick was pulsing at the thought of her. The scent that was all hers still in the room aggravated it even more.

"Okay. Love you."

Jeremiah waited for a long moment until he was sure whomever had been on the other side of the door was long gone and he slipped out of the room. He couldn't wait for them to come back to the hospital. He only had about four more hours before he needed to get back on the road. Fifteen minutes later, he was back in the Hummer and flooring it to Angel's, his thoughts on his strong, sexy mate. Damn, he needed her. He didn't know how much longer he could stay away.

He made it in record time, parking five miles away and hoofing it through the woods that surrounded the area. Confident they wouldn't be able to sense him with their psychic abilities, or scent his presence because of the pills he'd taken, Jeremiah got within half a mile of the farm before climbing up to the top of a tree and settling in. He was on a hill and had a direct view of the farm below him. Removing his backpack, he took out a pair of binoculars, anxious to see the mate he would do anything for. He paused, briefly having the presence of mind to inhale deeply and make sure he was alone, then put the binoculars to his eyes. It took him a moment to focus them in, and then his eyes widened at the frenzied fight that was taking place below him in front of the barn. Holy shit! If the female wolf was the one the person in the hospital had been talking about, she was right. Not only was the wolf angry, but she was fighting against a huge male for all she was worth. And she was winning.

The team surrounded them, but were keeping their distance. As Jeremiah watched, Nico quickly shed his clothes and shifted, and then he jumped into the fray. The female wolf, her fur full of beautiful brown and black colors, let go of the first threat to take on the new one.

Jeremiah tried to get a better look at her, but she was moving too fast. Who the hell was she?

Finally, pulling his gaze from the dizzy speed of the fighting wolves, he slowly tracked his way around the circle, looking for his Rikki. She wasn't there. He frowned, looking again, and then skimmed the binoculars over every portion of the farm that he could see from where he was. She wasn't in sight. Maybe she was in the barn?

His gaze going back to the crazy ass fight taking place, Jeremiah decided he was glad Rikki wasn't anywhere near it. He didn't know who the female wolf was that wasn't afraid to take on two male wolves at one time, but he didn't want his mate in the middle of it. He knew Rikki was strong, but there was something about the female below. She seemed half-wild, and when the males stepped back, she paused and raised her head. The pain and misery he saw in her dark brown eyes floored him. She was hurting so much.

Jeremiah watched the two males slowly start circling the female as she stood still, her sides heaving, her head lowered. She wasn't done, though. He could tell by the way her eyes tracked the other two. Nico crouched, growling in warning, and she bared her teeth at him. No, she wasn't done yet.

The female let out a loud howl and then sprang, tackling the other male wolf to the ground. She was on him, her teeth at his throat, when Chase rushed in and grabbed her around the middle, dragging her away and tossing her from him. Jeremiah could tell the White River Wolves alpha was mad as hell.

"Chase, no!"

He heard Angel's loud cry of agony all of the way from where he was.

"Rikki, you have to stop!"

Rikki?

The female wolf snarled, turning to where Chase was now removing his jeans. Throwing back her head, she howled again, and Jeremiah could hear the pain in that howl. She was suffering and acting out in the only way she could. The beast inside of him came to attention, and he froze. Rikki?

The two male wolves shifted quickly, and suddenly Nico and Phoenix were standing protectively in front of the female, their hands raised as they tried to reason with the alpha. He was having none of it.

"She's dangerous," Chase roared. "If the two of you together can't control her, I will!"

Jeremiah heard the anger in the alpha's voice and felt something he hadn't felt in years. Fear. Leaping from the tree limb he was sitting on to the ground below, he raced toward them. Rikki? No, it couldn't be.

"She's upset, Chase. She's been through so much."

Jeremiah could hear Angel pleading with her mate, but all he could think about was the wolf...and Rikki. Was it really her? And if so, how?

"She's a fucking menace," Chase snarled, as Jeremiah broke through the trees. "She's going to hurt someone. She needs to be stopped. Now."

Chase shifted and was on the female wolf before they could reply. She fought him, biting, tearing him with her claws, but she was no match for the alpha. In his mind, Jeremiah knew Chase was trying to protect the others, including his mate. A shifter would do anything for their mate. But once Jeremiah got a whiff of the female wolf, there was nothing stopping him. He had no idea how, but it was his Rikki! His claws broke free and he quickly shredded his clothes. Within seconds he and his bear had become one, and he was roaring a challenge to the alpha. He didn't give a fuck who the man was. No one touched his mate.

"Holy shit!"

"Oh, my God! It's a freaking bear!"

"Chase! Get away from Rikki! Hurry! It's Jeremiah!"

Jeremiah heard them all, but he didn't stop. A small trickle of blood could be seen from a wound in Rikki's side, one caused by the wolf who stood over her, swinging his large head in Jeremiah's direction. When the smell of his mate's blood hit him, Jeremiah let out another loud bellow.

"That is one pissed-off bear!"

"You would be, too, if you saw your mate pinned to the ground and bleeding."

"It's just a scratch."

"Still smells like blood. To a shifter, that shit's potent when it belongs to his mate."

"Jeremiah, stop!"

He ignored it all. He was on Chase, batting at him hard with a large paw, flinging the alpha away from the small female wolf. Standing over her, he roared his rage to all. Chase rose to his feet, snarling in anger as he began to advance toward them.

"Dammit, Chase. You need to calm down and back the hell off!" Angel yelled. "You are only making things worse. That's Jeremiah, Rikki's mate. He's just protecting her, like you were me." Angel ran between them, grabbing Chase, wrapping her arms tightly around his neck when he would have went passed her. "Stop, please."

Chase paused, lifting his head and howling his anger. Jeremiah knew if the alpha wanted to get to them, he would, but after a moment, Chase rubbed his head against his mate's arm, then pulled back from her. Shifting, he growled, "Get control of your mate, bear, or I will do it for you."

Jeremiah bared huge fangs at him, snarling, his large claws digging into the dirt as he fought the urge to go finish what he'd started. The son of a bitch had hurt his mate. Drew blood. She'd been hurt so much in her life. She deserved better. Raising himself to his full height, he roared loudly again.

"All right. We got it, big guy." His gaze swung to the redhead and he growled, low and deadly. "No one is going to lay a hand on your mate now that you are here. And, now, maybe she won't feel the need to gut us all."

His lip curled up, showing a large fang, and he growled again. Damn right no one was touching his woman. He would tear them apart, he didn't care who they were.

"Jeremiah?"

Rikki's voice broke through the red haze of rage in him, and he lowered his massive head to look down at her. Her beautiful brown eyes were wide in wonder, her dark hair lay in a halo around her head. She was so tiny compared to his bear, but she wasn't afraid.

Slowly, she reached up and trailed a hand over the side of his head and down his face before tears filled her eyes. "You didn't come back to me. Why didn't you come back?"

He could hear the hurt in her voice, scent the pain she

felt. So much of it. At that moment, he realized this was his fault. He was the cause of her anger, her pain, her fighting against the people she loved.

"I needed you," she whispered. "It was so dark. So lonely. Where were you?"

Her suffering nearly suffocated him. He had no idea what she was talking about. Dark? What did she mean? And how was she suddenly a wolf? She was supposed to be a bear, dammit. His bear.

"Don't you want me?"

Did he want her? Hell, more than anything in the world. Leaning down, he inhaled deeply. Her scent had changed some, which he knew was because of her wolf, but she was still his Rikki. Still his mate. Chuffing softly, he buried his snout in her neck, inhaling again. His.

"I need to put some clothes on," Rikki whispered, pushing at him as she glanced furtively around. He growled, raising his eyes to look at everyone staring at them. "Please, Jeremiah. I don't want them to see me like this."

Surprised at the vulnerability in her voice, he lowered his body, covering hers with his, careful not to put any of his weight on her, as he growled in warning at everyone who was still standing there staring at them. Rikki was uncomfortable, and that upset his bear. Glaring at them, he growled again.

"Get Rikki's clothes. And a bandage to coverup that cut until it can be cleaned," Angel ordered, her hand clutching tightly to Chase's arm. The shifter stood, tall and proud, his dick hanging out for all to see, and for some reason that pissed Jeremiah off even more. His mate didn't need to see any other male's junk. When Jeremiah growled again, his gaze on Chase's lower half, Angel grinned. "I think he wants you to put some pants on, mate."

Shaking his head, Chase leaned down to kiss her quickly before stalking over to where he'd left his clothes. "Fucking pants. Maybe he should be thinking about what he's going to wear since he shredded all of his clothing."

"I got him a pair of mine from the truck," Steele said, striding over to where Jeremiah still crouched over Rikki, stopping a few feet from them to toss over the jogging pants. "Good to see you again, bear. I'll never forget the way you treated me in Alaska. As if I were a person instead of a thing. Nor will I forget how you let us go, even giving us a means of transportation. I am in your debt."

Jeremiah let his gaze roam over the man for a moment, before he grunted in acknowledgment. He remembered him. The assholes in the Alaska facility had taken pleasure in carving off his skin a couple of times a week, along with other experiments. He hated the way the shifter was treated and had shown him more than one act of kindness. Something he did to several of the prisoners when he was sure he wouldn't get caught.

"Here you go." It was the redhead again. He wasn't sure who she was, although she did look familiar, but it seemed as if she were a part of the team now. She sat Rikki's clothes down near them, along with a large bandage she must have gotten from a first aid box in the barn, before slowly backing away.

"Thank you, Flame," Rikki said quietly.

"We're going into the house," Angel told them. "Meet

us in the conference room once you're dressed and ready." They all left without another word.

Jeremiah watched them intently, waiting until the door to the house banged shut after the last one, before he looked back down at his mate. She stared at him, her eyes wide and glistening with unshed tears and something else. His mate was angry. Only, this time, it was at him.

Burying his huge head in between her shoulder and neck once again, he said a quick prayer that she would forgive him, and then shifted.

9

R ikki bit her lip, clamping down hard on the tears that wanted to fall. What was wrong with her? Her emotions were like a rollercoaster, up and down and just all over the place. No matter what she did, she couldn't seem to get control over them or her wolf.

She swallowed hard when Jeremiah lifted his head, and she found herself staring into a pair of intent, dark eyes fringed with a pair of the longest lashes she'd ever seen on a man. Dark brown hair with lighter brown highlights, a strong nose, hard lips, a jaw made of granite. Rikki's wolf whimpered in the back of her mind as his scent enveloped her, flowing through her. She felt her fangs drop, and a shudder ran through her. Mine!

"Hey," he said gruffly, his gaze tracing over her face.

Rikki closed her eyes, her breath coming in small pants as she fought the urge to sink her teeth deep into the flesh on his shoulder. Her body felt feverish; she trembled at the feel of his skin against hers. All over. They were naked, and she was on fire. Her nipples beaded up, and a moan slipped free when he moved, his hard cock pressing into her thigh.

"Rikki, look at me."

Hell, no. He was not ordering her around. She gave him what he wanted, but only partly. Opening her eyes, she glared at him and snapped, "You left me, Jeremiah Black! Not only that, but you knew we were mates years ago and did absolutely nothing about it. You don't have the right to tell me what to do now."

His eyes softened, and he lowered his head, rubbing his cheek over hers. "I'm sorry, baby. I should have said something, but I didn't think you were ready for me."

"Why do you think you get to decide what I'm ready for and when?" she growled, shoving at his huge chest, biting back a groan at the feel of his coarse chest hair on the palms of her hands. Why did she like that so much? "Get off me, you big oaf!"

"Rikki, I'm sorry."

"You should be!"

She tried to shove him off her again, but when he didn't budge, she began to struggle beneath him. The brush of his skin against hers had her wanting things she shouldn't, and that just made her angry. Yes, he was her mate, but he had left her, dammit!

"Baby, you need to stop," Jeremiah growled, groaning into her neck. "I swear, my cock is fucking hard as hell right now. You keep moving like that, I'm going to come all over like a damn teenager."

Rikki gasped at the dark edge of desire in Jeremiah's tone, arching up into him before she could stop herself. He was so hard all over; his chest, his abs, his hips, his thighs, and yes, that long, thick cock pressing into her. She could feel all of him, and she wanted it. All. Too bad that was impossible. She needed some answers first.

Gritting her teeth, Rikki nudged her knee in between his legs, tangled her ankles with his, and shoved hard at his chest while pushing with her legs. She heard his grunt of surprise when she flipped him over onto his back, and then she was scrambling to her feet, moving quickly away from him. "You don't have the right to touch me, either," she snarled, finding her clothes and quickly yanking them on, wincing when her hand brushed against the cut on her side. "As a matter of fact, you have no rights to me whatsoever."

She heard him moving, but refused to look in his direction until she was fully dressed. She needed some kind of armor between them, and right now, all she had were the thin pieces of threads covering her body. Finally, when she glanced over at him, she found him dressed in the jogging pants Steele had brought him, along with a tight, black tee shirt that accented the hard muscles on his chest. It would seem Steele had brought him more than just pants. Rikki wasn't sure if it was a blessing or not. Silently, he held out the bandage to her, obviously smart enough to know when to stay back.

"Baby..."

"Stop calling me that," she snapped, snatching it from him, her hands going to her hips as she glared at him. "If I was your anything, you would have been here these past five months when I was lying in a hospital bed after I almost died!"

"What the fuck are you talking about?" he snarled,

taking a step closer to her, his eyes darkening in anger. "What do you mean, you almost died?"

By the look on his face, she could tell Jeremiah had no idea what happened to her back in January. She almost softened to him... almost. Until she thought about the fact that if he had bothered to check in on her just once, he would have known. "In all this time, you haven't even made a phone call to see how I'm doing, Jeremiah? I thought that's what mates did? Love, cherish, protect. I've seen the way the White River Wolves are with their mates. The way my team members are. And you couldn't even pick up a phone to call?"

"Dammit, Rikki. I *was* protecting you! The General's men don't mess around. If I placed a call and they traced it back to you, what do you think would have happened? One phone call could have gotten both of us killed."

She knew he was right, but what about before then? He'd known she was his for years, ever since they first met when he was giving them missions, but not once had he said anything to her. He'd kept her in the dark about their mating, and when she found out, he still didn't follow through with anything. Instead, he just disappeared. Shaking her head in frustration, she ripped open the bandage, slid up her shirt, and slapped it on, hissing in pain.

"Rikki." Her name was a whisper on his lips as Jeremiah slowly closed the distance between them. Clenching her teeth together, she glared at him, wanting his touch, but also wanting to push him away. Reaching out, he traced his fingers down her face before cupping her cheek in the palm of his hand. "I know you don't understand why I did what I did, and maybe you never will. I would like the chance to explain, though. Give me that at least."

One of the tears she'd held in for so long slipped out, sliding down her cheek onto his hand.

"Ah, baby, please don't cry."

A shudder ran through her when he leaned in and kissed the tear away.

"You are everything to me, Rikki Diamond. My heart, world. You own me. If you want me to get out, I will. Right now. This minute. I'll fight the fight from here with you."

Rikki's heart skipped a beat, and she stared into his dark eyes, hope becoming a small light in her chest. "You will?"

"Yeah," he promised gruffly. "Don't you know? I would do anything for you."

Jeremiah lowered his head toward hers, and Rikki gasped when their lips met. Her hands went to his chest, clutching tightly to his shirt as her whole body began to tremble. She felt his tongue touch the seam of her mouth, and she opened, letting him slip inside. He groaned, his tongue thrusting past her lips to find and tangle with her own. That fire was back, racing through her veins. Her breath came in short pants, a moan crawling up her throat. His arm wrapped around her waist, pulling her into him, flush against his body. His hard cock against her stomach, and she wondered what it would feel like to have it inside of her. She'd only had sex once in her life. It had left a lot to be desired. But the way Jeremiah made her feel, she knew it wouldn't be the same with him. She wanted to find out so bad, but they had a lot they needed to get through before she could. That didn't mean she couldn't play some now, though.

Sliding her hands up his chest, she sank them into his thick hair, loving the texture against her skin. She froze, suddenly realizing she wasn't wearing her gloves. The ones she wore all of the time to keep the whispers from past, present, and future away. But, there was nothing, when there should have been. Nothing from the clothes Jeremiah was wearing, nor from his skin or hair. Nothing. She didn't understand it, but she reveled in it. Normally, she was unable to touch anything without getting some sort of reading off of it. Now, she was putting her hands all over her mate, and it was heaven.

"Fuck, Rikki, I've missed you so much."

The growled words against her mouth pulled her from her haze of desire. She'd missed him, too. Even in her coma, she had somehow known he wasn't there. Felt it. She was so lost and alone, struggling to find her way back to the land of the living. Rikki remembered everything, and it hurt.

As if sensing her change of mood, Jeremiah gave her one last small kiss and then rested his cheek against hers. "We have lot to talk about."

"Yes."

"Promise me, you will give me a chance to explain everything. I've waited too long for you to lose you now."

Rikki sighed, trying to let go of some of the anger she had bottled up. It was tearing her up inside, and affecting not only her, but everyone around her. Shame filled her at the thought of what she'd done to her brothers. She'd drawn blood, and that was unacceptable. She had a lot to

RARE 71

apologize for. She would be a hypocrite not to listen to Jeremiah after everything she'd done on her end.

"We need to meet with the team now," she whispered, stepping back from him.

"After?"

Rikki hesitated before nodding. "After."

10

Jeremiah followed his mate down the stairs to where he knew the conference room was in Angel's home. She'd promised to talk to him after the meeting, but that was all she was giving him right now. He would take it. He had screwed up. Everything he did, he did for her, but she was right. He should have found a way to check on her in the past few months. It didn't matter how deep undercover he was, he should have done something. She was his mate, the most important person in his life. Sighing, he shook his head. He should have done a lot of things, but it was too late for that now. Rikki had almost died, and where was he? Not with her where he belonged. That was going to change. Fuck Ebony and the rest of the organization. His mate needed him, and he wasn't leaving her.

Angel glanced up from a map she was looking at when they walked in. It looked like the schematics of a building, and the layout looked familiar at first glance. His gaze went to the men and women in the room. It seemed much more crowded than the last time he was down there. His thoughts went to the reason he'd been there before, and a low growl slipped free. His mate had been kidnapped by the General's men, and he'd sworn then that no one would ever get to her again. He'd been wrong.

When Rikki looked back at him, an eyebrow raised, he shook his head, not wanting to explain himself in front of everyone. The thought of his mate taken by that bastard made him want to somehow bring him back to life so he could kill him again. But he didn't need everyone in the room to know where his thoughts had gone.

Jeremiah leaned up against a wall just inside the doorway, his hand going to Rikki's hip to pull her gently back against him. He was grateful when she didn't fight him. He needed to feel her close. Bowing his head, he closed his eyes and inhaled her scent again. Sweet, feminine, his.

"How long do you have, Jeremiah?"

His hand tightening on Rikki's hip, Jeremiah raised his head to look at Angel. "I'm not going anywhere."

She frowned in confusion. "Aren't they expecting you somewhere? I wasn't aware the General," she paused, "I mean, Ebony, gave vacation days?"

Jeremiah shrugged. "She doesn't."

A slow smile crossed the alpha's lips and she nodded. "Good. It's about time you came home."

Jeremiah felt Rikki relax against him, and he slid an arm around her waist. "It's where I need to be."

"I'm not so sure about that, bear."

Jeremiah stiffened when Jinx appeared at the door. Showing his fangs, he growled, "I'm not leaving my mate."

Jinx's gaze went to Rikki, and one of his rare grins

appeared. "Hey, little wolf. It's good to see you out of that damn hospital bed."

"You knew about all of this and didn't tell me?" Jeremiah snarled, careful not to pinch Rikki with his large claws that sprang free as anger raced through him.

"Jinx saved my life," Rikki said softly.

Jeremiah frowned, leaning down to inhale her scent again. He caught nothing of the male on her. "He didn't turn you."

"No," Jinx agreed, sending Rikki another gentle smile. Jeremiah had never seen the man smile before, and he wasn't sure he liked it directed at his mate. Jinx laughed when Jeremiah bared his teeth at him again, but the laughter didn't meet his eyes. "Rikki was shot by one of the General's men. It severed an artery, almost killing her. I was able to fix it, but she never would have lived if Angel hadn't changed her."

Angel. Jeremiah shot the woman a grateful look before saying, "I didn't know anyone but a mate could turn someone."

"A very strong alpha can."

"Thank the Gods above I was strong enough," Angel said quietly.

"I knew you would be." Jinx glanced around the room, not leaving the open doorway. "Vixen isn't here yet?"

"You told that woman where this place is?" Angel growled, rising from her seat.

"You're going to have to trust her at some point," Jinx said with a shrug.

"Who says?" Angel snarled, her hands on her hips as she glared at her son.

"Me."

Angel's eyes narrowed, and she glanced down at Chase, before looking back at Jinx. "Is there a reason?"

"She can be trusted," Jinx said simply.

"Why do I have a feeling this fun little convo is about me?"

It was a voice he knew, one he'd heard many times when he'd worked at the Virginia facility. Jeremiah's eyes widened when Jinx stepped to the side and one of the General's assassins walked into the room. "What the hell is she doing here?" he snarled, quickly moving to stand in front of his mate.

"I could ask the same of you," Vixen said, raising a delicate eyebrow as she glanced in his direction. "Seems like there are lots of secrets going on around here."

When Rikki tried to step around him, Jeremiah kept her back with an arm, his gaze never leaving the woman who was just a few feet away. "Explain yourself, now," he snarled. "I have no problem dispensing of one of the General's lackeys. I don't care who you know."

Vixen laughed, the sound floating around the room and pissing him off more. "Lackey? Like you, you mean?"

"Jeremiah is one of us," Chase said, rising to stand beside his mate. "Tell us, Vixen, what are you doing here?"

"I was invited," the woman said with a shrug, and a glance over at Jinx. "If you don't want me here, I can leave. But I infiltrate in twenty-four hours by myself, then."

"Infiltrate where?"

"The facility in Virginia. Ebony has decided to get rid of it and everyone in it. It being my home base, I've grown attached to a few of the people there. I would rather they live."

"I don't understand," Rikki said, slamming her elbow

in Jeremiah's ribs to try to get him to move. "Who are you?"

Jeremiah refused to budge. He didn't want Rikki anywhere near the bitch in front of him. He'd seen first-hand what she was capable of.

"She's one of the General's assassins."

"Oh!" Rikki stopped struggling, her hand resting on his back. "Like Jinx."

The subtle reminder was quiet in the room, and Jeremiah felt pride fill him at what his mate was conveying in those two words. She was trying to tell him that he needed to get his head out of his ass and see the big picture. Jinx wouldn't have brought her to the meeting if she couldn't be trusted. But trust had to be earned, and Vixen sure as hell hadn't earned his. Neither he, nor his bear were on board with her being there.

"Like me," Jinx agreed, moving to block the doorway again. "And she's here of her own free will. She's asking for help. We are."

"Talk to us," Angel demanded, taking her seat at the table again, Chase sitting beside her. Theirs was a well-matched mating, full of a shared power like nothing Jeremiah had ever felt before between an alpha pair.

"I found out last night that Ebony has planned to eliminate everyone at the Virginia facility," Jinx started, his gaze going around the room. "She knows there is a leak somewhere and assumes part of it was Vixen."

"Since I was out of the Virginia facility, she's decided she can't trust anyone there," Vixen spat, her eyes taking on an angry glow. "That bitch needs to die."

Jeremiah ignored the snarls of agreement in the room, one thing standing out to him. "They were sending me to

Virginia. I thought it odd, because they were having me drive a Hummer there when normally they would fly."

"They are tracking you," Vixen said immediately.

"I disabled the tracking device on the vehicle."

"Your phone."

"Left it behind in the garage. Made it look like I dropped it on accident."

Vixen grinned, "Then, unless you've been to sickbay recently, you should be fine."

"Never been," Jeremiah told her. "Why?"

"They've started embedding small tracking devices into the base of the neck of the guards, right under the skin."

"I've never heard that," Jeremiah snarled.

"It's something new," Vixen told them, with a shrug. "So small, you wouldn't even know it. One of the scientists in a facility in California has been working on it for the past four or five years. From what I've been told, it hurts like hell when they inject it into you, but then the pain goes away after a few days. They haven't figured out a way to make it painless when they shoot it into you. You would know if you have one."

"I don't." Thank fuck. He couldn't stand the thought of having something injected into him so he could be watched at all times.

"They probably didn't want to waste one on you, since they were obviously sending you to your death anyway," Vixen said as she began to pace the small confines of the room. "They are very expensive to make."

Jeremiah stiffened, and a low growl filled the room from behind him. "Sending me to my death?"

"Well, you just said you were going to the Virginia

facility. Why else would they send you there if not to kill you? There are kill orders on everyone there. Guards, scientists, shifters. Why would you be any different?"

He wouldn't. The realization that they must have finally figured out he was in their organization under-cover sank in, and he slowly turned to slide an arm around Rikki, bringing her up next to him. "Guess it's a good thing I'm not going back."

"That's the problem. We need you to."

"No fucking way," Rikki snarled, her eyes going wolf as she glared at the woman. "He isn't going anywhere near that place. You'll have to go through me first."

Vixen's gaze raked over her, and a slow smile slipped free. "I haven't had a good fight since Jinx. As much fun as that would be, though, we don't have time. We need to get this shit figured out. Fast."

"Well, you are going to figure it out without putting my mate in more danger," Rikki growled.

"Mate? Interesting. What's it like having a mate? I've always wondered, but only one of the shifters I met in Virginia was mated, and she refused to tell me any specifics about it."

"What? Which one has a mate?" Jeremiah asked, horror filling him at the thought of what they and their mate must be going through. Staying away from Rikki had been hell, and they weren't even fully mated, yet.

"Jasmine, the fox shifter."

"Shit."

"Yeah, for just over a couple of years now. We need to get her out of there. I may not know a lot about what being mated to someone means, but I do understand that mates can't survive without one another."

"They can," Angel admitted, "but it's a hell no one wants to live."

"She has a baby," Vixen said quietly, turning to look at Jeremiah. "Just a year old. I know you don't want to go back in, and I wouldn't ask it of you if I didn't need someone on the inside, but I promised Jasmine I would get her back to her family. Back to her baby. She wouldn't tell me much, but she did talk about little Shayla sometimes. Said she missed her so much she could hardly breath." Her gaze went to Rikki, and she whispered, "I don't ask for much. I don't like to rely on others, but I'm asking you, please help me save her. Help me get her back to her baby. I honestly don't know if I can do it on my own. They would have changed the security codes when I went missing. Locked down tighter on security."

It felt as if a weight had settled on Jeremiah's chest. He knew Vixen told the truth, could scent it. There was no acrid odor of a lie, and the pain he felt coming from her was real. It surprised him. Shocked the hell out of him. He hadn't thought the General's assassins could feel. He'd been wrong.

Rikki turned in his arms, looking up to meet his eyes. Hers were wide and misted over with tears. He saw the indecision within them, the same indecision he felt. "You have to go back," she whispered, her hand coming up to rest on his cheek. "You don't have a choice."

"I can't leave you." It was torn from him, and he didn't care who heard the guttural pain in his voice. He had been away from his mate for too long. He didn't want to be separated from her again.

"You won't," she promised, leaning into him. "We will be right there with you."

"She's right," Angel vowed. "We will be there, and as soon as you give us the signal, we will come in, guns blazing. We will get that little fox back to her mate and baby, and we will bring you home."

Closing his eyes, Jeremiah wrapped his arms around Rikki, holding her close. Resting his forehead on the top of her head, he muttered, "I promised you I wouldn't go away again."

"You aren't leaving me," Rikki whispered. "We are in this together this time."

Swallowing hard, he raised his head to look at Angel. "I need to be to Virginia by tomorrow afternoon. I will need to leave immediately."

"Let me help with that," Jinx cut in. "You stay a bit longer with Rikki. Angel can fly you in with them, and I will meet you close to the facility with the Hummer."

"Thanks, man."

Rikki turned to look at the young shifter, her arms tightening around Jeremiah's waist before she whispered, "Thank you, Jinx."

"You're pack. It's what pack does."

He felt Rikki stiffen in his arms as her gaze went to Chase and Angel. "It seems I have a lot to learn about being part of a pack."

"Don't worry, little wolf," Chase said, a small smile kicking up the corners of his mouth. "You have time."

"I thought you wanted to eliminate me," she whispered. "You said I was a menace."

Chase rose, crossing the room to them. Jeremiah could feel the alpha sending some of his power to Rikki, letting it run through her and relax her. "I never said I wanted to eliminate you, Rikki. I just wanted you to get your wolf under control. You were hurting people."

Rikki bowed her head in shame. "I don't want to hurt anyone. I was just in so much pain, and so angry."

Chase settled a hand gently on the top of her head. "You are our family, Rikki. Even if you haven't accepted me yet, you are one of my wolves to protect. I take that very seriously."

"You were trying to protect me, along with everyone else?"

"I will always be here to protect you," he promised. "Even if it is from yourself."

Jeremiah watched as his mate raised her head, a tremulous smile crossing her lips. "Thank you."

"Yes, Alpha," he said, holding out a hand to Chase. "Thank you for claiming my mate as one of yours and protecting her. Keeping her safe."

"Always," Chase promised, sliding his hand in Jeremiah's. "That extends to you, too, Jeremiah. You are Rikki's mate, which makes you family. Mine to protect."

Jeremiah bowed his head to the man, baring his neck in deference to the alpha. He knew he was being bestowed a great honor. It was a huge blessing, and one he did not take lightly. "Thank you, Alpha."

BANE STOOD on the edge of Angel's property, his gaze surveying as far out as the eye could see. She was out there somewhere, probably terrified, fighting for her life, and there wasn't a damn thing he could do about it. It was driving him crazy. He'd never even met her before. The others had, but he'd stayed behind to help guard the White River Wolves when they were out on missions where they ran into her. The General's daughter. Amber. He still couldn't wrap his mind around it. He was mated to the spawn of Satan. He still hated the bastard, even though he was dead. Everyone said Amber was nothing like her father or her sister, Ebony. That she was kind, good, and would give her life to protect the people the General and Ebony held captive. Possibly already had. He wanted to believe them. Wanted to believe his mate had a kind, gentle soul and a good heart. But she'd been born into a family who liked to hurt and kill. How could she be so different? The General had ruined his life. How could he forget that? He knew Amber wasn't responsible for her father's actions, but… how?

Bane squeezed the bridge of his nose with his thumb and forefinger, closing his eyes as he thought back to how his world had changed so long ago. The General had taken his brother from them, making him do unthinkable things. When the bastard tried to make him choose between his family and pack or his children, there had been only one choice Steele could make. Because of it, the bastard came back and murdered everyone in their pack except for himself and his sister, Sapphire, who had managed to escape after killing several of the General's men. After that, Bane had become a whole new person. No longer was he the outgoing son who loved to spend his time reading and teasing his sister. His father used to tell him that he couldn't fight a war with words. He had naively responded, "Watch me." After the loss of their entire village, he realized that wasn't true. That he was living in a dream world, and it was time to wake up. He began to train hard, learning to use everything he had at his disposal to defeat the enemy. He ran, lifted weights, shifted several times a day so that he could increase the speed in which he changed. He could shoot almost as well as Sapphire, fight dirty as hell with a knife, take down a bear if he had to. He also had the ability to speak telepathically, along with a couple other gifts he kept close to his chest. Only Sapphire knew all of the things he could do, and he was keeping it that way, for now.

His thoughts went back to his mate, and he once again raised his head to look out over the land. Where was she? Was she alive? Hell, was she evil or the fucking angel everyone said she was?

"You have to stop, brother." Sapphire appeared beside him, sliding her arm through the crook in his. "It's tearing you up inside." When he didn't reply, she laid her head on his shoulder. "You know the girl can't help who she's related to. We don't get to pick our family. Well, not our biological one, anyway."

"I know," he muttered.

"Then, why are you holding that against her? Why not believe what the entire team is telling you? What your own sister is telling you? That she is a woman worthy of you."

"Because," he rasped, placing a hand on top of hers and squeezing gently. "If I do, that means I have to think about the fact that my mate, who is by everyone's standards an angel from above, is being held and possibly tortured by her own sister. I don't know which would be worse, Sapphire. Believing she is the embodiment of evil and finding out later that I'm wrong. Or believing she is everything that is good in this world, and finding her used and abused, a shell of the person she used to be."

Sapphire sighed, running a hand gently down his arm. "All I can tell you is what I saw personally, Bane. I saw her stand between Chase and the bastard who was trying to kill him. She was willing to die so that he could live. I saw her leave, walk back into the hell that was waiting for her, to save the people the General was holding prisoner. I saw her courage, but also her fear."

Bane swallowed hard, gritting his teeth tightly together. "She's strong," he got out, but barely.

"Did you know that Chase has claimed her as one of his?"

Bane shook his head, staring straight ahead as his eyes misted over with tears. Dammit, he was a man. Men didn't cry.

"So has Angel. They say Amber is family." Hugging his arm to her, Sapphire said, "They did this before they knew she was yours. Bane, she may be the daughter of the devil, but she is not him. She is worthy of your claim. Worthy of your love. You need to put aside your hatred for a dead man and concentrate on what really matters."

"Amber." Bane could barely breathe, the thought of his mate, a woman he wanted to hate but couldn't, in the hands of someone like Ebony. "How do we find her?"

"I've been trying ever since she was taken." The voice was deep, low, family.

Bane pulled away from Sapphire and turned to look at his nephew. Jinx. One of the General's assassins. Proof you could live in the face of adversity and overcome it all. He was raised to be a killer. Taught in depth how to fight, torture, and kill. He'd lived his entire life with only his father and sister as a positive influence, until the year before when he met his mother and RARE, and he still turned out to be someone Bane could be proud of. He may kill for Ebony, but he saved as many lives as he took, if not more. Bane would trust the man with his life. He was proof Amber could be as kind and caring as everyone believed her to be. And if she was, that meant his mate was going through a hell that could kill her right now because Ebony would never allow her to survive.

"She is," Jinx said quietly.

"Is what?" Bane asked, even though he knew the answer. With ever fiber of his being, he knew what Jinx was going to say.

"Amber is good, kind, caring. A woman to be proud of. If she were mine, I wouldn't be standing here fucking debating about whether or not she was worthy of my love. I would know it, because my father told me the Gods would never give us a mate who was unworthy of us. I've seen the mated pairs around here, and I believe him. I wouldn't be arguing with myself over whether or not I could learn to love someone like the General's daughter. I would be moving heaven and earth to find the other half of my soul, knowing she would make me whole. Something I've never been."

Bane stared into his nephew's eyes, eyes that they were now glowing a bright green when just moments ago they'd been a deep brown like his own. A good indicator that the man was pissed. Bane sighed, raking a hand through his hair. Jinx was right, and he had just effectively put his uncle in his place. "I'm an ass."

Jinx didn't argue, his jaw hard, his eyes taking on another hue of green. "Amber gives and gives to everyone else, never asking for anything in return. She put her life on the line numerous times, trying to free the General's prisoners, or, at least, make their lives less miserable when she could. She knew what could happen to her if she got caught. What *would* happen. She did it anyway. She has more heart and soul than anyone else I know."

"Point taken." Bane rubbed at the ache in his chest, agony strumming through him at the thought of what Amber might be going through now. "You have no idea where she is?"

"No," Jinx growled, looking away from him. "Ebony won't tell me, and she has her mind locked down too damn tight for me to get in."

"Get me near her," Bane said, crossing his arms over his chest. "She won't be able to hide the truth from me."

"Bane…" Sapphire whispered, taking a step forward and placing a hand on his arm. "We talked about this. There has to be another way."

"I'll make it quick," Bane promised, his eyes never leaving his nephew's. "Get me near her."

Jinx nodded slowly, his eyes widening slightly.

"Jinx?"

"Yeah?"

"Stay the fuck out of my head unless I invite you in." Bane's voice was cold, deadly. He would never hurt his nephew, but he would show the boy some manners, if he needed to.

Jinx grinned, throwing him a salute as he turned to walk away.

"Get me near her, Jinx."

Jinx raised a hand, then took off at a jog through the forest of trees in the back of Angel's property.

"You sure about this?"

Bane turned back to look out over the horizon, nodding slowly. He wondered if it was telling that his gaze kept going to the southeast. Was his mate in that direction? Hopefully, he would find out soon. "Yeah, I'm sure." If it was the only way to find Amber, he didn't have a choice.

R ikki stood in the shower, letting the water cascade over her as tears ran down her cheeks. Her emotions were in an upheaval, and there didn't seem to be a damn thing she could do about it. She couldn't blame it on her wolf this time, though. No, this time it was all her. The female who didn't want to send her male back into hell, knowing he may not come out again. She had agreed that Jeremiah needed to go to Virginia, had even encouraged it, but her heart was breaking at the thought of what could happen when he got there. Even knowing she and the team would be right outside the facility, waiting for his command to infiltrate, didn't make it better. Anything could happen. She could lose her mate before she even had a chance to claim him.

"Baby, you have to stop. Your tears are killing me."

Rikki was aware of the shower curtain being pulled back, and then the water was shut off. A large towel was wrapped around her, and then she was being lifted very gently into a pair of strong arms. Jeremiah's arms. Laying her head against his thick chest, she inhaled deeply, taking his scent deep inside her.

"I won't go," he muttered, rubbing his cheek against hers as he walked into the bedroom at Angel's farm that she was using for now. "We'll find another way."

"There is no other way," she whispered, her tears falling on his skin. "We both know that."

"There's always another way. We just have to find it."

Raising her head, she looked into his dark eyes. Eyes full of compassion, and something else that made her breath catch. For her. Laying a hand on his cheek, she forced herself to give him a small smile. "It will be too late for Jasmine by then, and you know it. This is the only way to get in quickly enough to free her and the others. She has a mate, a child. I can't let myself be selfish, no matter how much I may want to."

Jeremiah's deep brown eyes darkened even more, and he slowly lowered her to her feet. "My Rikki," he said, as he began to gently run the towel over her body. "Always worried about others, never putting herself first." The towel glided over her chest, and then his mouth was following behind it. Rikki cried out at the sensations rushing through her as he licked over the curve of her breast, and then around her nipple, teasing it lightly before sucking it into the hot recesses of his mouth.

"Jeremiah!"

"My sweet mate," he rasped, moving the towel around to slide it over her back while his lips whispered across her skin to her other breast.

Rikki felt a small laugh slip free. "I don't think anyone has ever called me sweet before."

"Then, they don't know you very well." Jeremiah knelt

in front of her, and she shuddered when she felt the rasp of the towel over her buttocks. Gently, he kissed around the cut on her side that was already healing. "I should have hurt him, just a little."

"It's just a scratch," she breathed, her body trembling as he moved lower.

"Should have gutted him."

"You can't gut the alpha."

"Watch me." Rikki's laughter turned into a moan when his tongue swirled around her navel. "So sweet," he groaned, as he moved lower. "And all mine."

When his tongue stroked over her clit, Rikki cried out, pleasure swamping her. No one had ever touched her like this, kissed her the way he was. Jeremiah growled, sliding his tongue lower, over her wet folds, and she moaned his name as the sound vibrated through her. Sliding her hands into his thick hair, she fought to stay on her feet as her thighs began to shake uncontrollably. "Jeremiah! I don't know what to do," she admitted, moaning again when his tongue entered her. "It feels so good!"

Pulling back, he looked up at her, his eyes glowing bright as he licked his lips. "You taste so fucking good, baby."

Tightening her hands in his hair, she gasped when she felt him slide a finger deep inside her. "Jeremiah! I…" She didn't know what to say. Sensations were running wild within her, her body taut and alive, waiting for something.

"Just feel, Rikki," he said, as he added another finger, stretching her.

"Oh, God!"

"That's it," he growled, lowering his head and finding her clit again with his tongue. "All you need to do is feel."

The flick of his tongue against the small ball of nerves had her going crazy. Clutching at his head, she arched into him, screaming his name when it felt as if something exploded inside of her. It rushed through her, tearing down her defenses, leaving her weak against the onslaught of emotion surrounding her. The anger she held against him for staying away so long, the fear she felt that he wouldn't make it out of Virginia alive, the desire that consumed her when he touched her, the love she'd tried to hold back for so long. It all slammed into her as she exploded on his tongue, and she couldn't stop what happened next.

Her vision changed, and Rikki knew she was seeing through the eyes of her wolf. Her fangs dropped, and a deep growl emerged. "Mine," she snarled. Her hands dropped to Jeremiah's shoulders, her claws digging in deep.

"Rikki," he groaned, lifting his head to look at her. "Oh, fuck."

His eyes widened slightly, and then she was looking at his bear. His own fangs emerged, his breathing becoming labored as he rose quickly, sweeping her up into his arms and depositing her on the bed.

"Mine," she snarled again, watching as he slid out of the jogging pants he had on. Then he was on the bed with her, lying between her legs, his mouth on hers. Arching her hips up to meet his, she moaned when she felt the hardness of his cock between her thighs.

"Baby, are you sure? I don't think I can stop my bear from taking you. It's been so long. Too long."

Rikki felt the tension strumming through his body, which was covered in a thin layer of sweat. Low growls emitted from deep in his chest as he struggled to hold himself back. His forearms shook with the effort to hold himself above her. His fangs were large and long, and his eyes were glued to her shoulder, where she knew he wanted to leave his mark. Was she sure? She had wanted him for so long. She'd been angry at him for not claiming her long ago. For leaving her when she needed him most. For not being there when she woke up after the terror of being locked in darkness for months. But through it all, there was one thing she'd always known. He was hers, as she was his. That wasn't going to change no matter what else happened.

Slipping a hand down between them, she wrapped her fingers around his cock, reveling in the velvety soft skin that covered the rock hardness of him.

"Rikki."

Her name was a deep growl, and she could tell he was at the end of his control. Good, so was she. Guiding him to her entrance, she wrapped her legs around him, arching into him, pushing his cock inside. He was big, so long and thick, she had to take him slowly. Soon, he was filling her, snarling above her as he held himself in check. She didn't want him in control. She wanted him wild. She wanted so much.

Baring her teeth, she snarled, "Mine," once more before raising up and sinking her fangs deep into his shoulder. He was hers, dammit. Now and always. They would live together and die together. She was never letting him go again.

"Rikki!" She felt the moment when Jeremiah's control

snapped. One second he had a tight reign over it, and then it was just gone. Grasping one of her hips tightly, he shoved deep inside her, withdrew, and slammed in again. "Tell me I'm not hurting you," he groaned, his hips pistoning as he thrust deep inside her again and again. "Please, baby, I can't stop."

She growled against his shoulder, lifting her hips to meet him, thrust for thrust. He would never hurt her. "More!" she snarled, raking her claws down his back.

"Fuck!"

Jeremiah paused, lifting one of her legs to reposition them, and then began to move again. He was getting even deeper now, moving even faster, and she loved it. Letting go of his shoulder, she threw her head back and gave herself over to just feeling. It was like nothing she'd ever experienced before. The sensations running through her, the way her body hummed with excitement, it all swamped her, and soon she was going over the edge again, coming around his cock.

His eyes glowing brighter, Jeremiah bared his fangs. "Mine," he growled, his eyes locked to her shoulder.

"Do it," she snarled, arching her neck back. "Fucking do it!"

He struck, his fangs digging deep into her shoulder, and a loud roar filled the room as he came inside her. His body went taut, and he snarled and growled around his teeth.

"Yes!" Rikki cried out as she came again, pulsing around his cock. She felt the bond snap into place, one that could never be broken, not even in death. She was his, as he was hers. Their souls merged together. It was like nothing she'd ever felt before.

It was several minutes later before Jeremiah finally slid his teeth from Rikki's shoulder, licking at the mark as he slipped from inside her. Raising his head, he looked down at her, love shining from his eyes. "I think it's time we talked, little one."

Rikki raised her head and captured his mouth with hers before pulling back to whisper, "Yes, it is."

12

"You put your gloves back on," Jeremiah said quietly, tracing over her fingers lightly where they lay on his chest.

"I have to wear them. If I don't, I get too much energy off of everything I touch," Rikki explained, rubbing her cheek against his bare chest. She loved the way the hair on it tickled her skin.

"I don't understand."

Of course, he didn't. She knew he was aware of some of their gifts, but not all of them. RARE kept that information as tightly under wraps as possible. If it got out, it would be dangerous to all of them.

"When I touch things — mostly objects — I get images. Visions. It could be of the past, present, or future. Sometimes, it's hard to figure out which one it is." She waited for him to say something, but when he didn't, she went on, "When I was young, it was hard to control. In one of the foster homes I was in when I was about eight, I touched a beer bottle my foster dad wanted me to throw in the trash. I got this flash of him using his fists on one of the children there. I told the social worker when she came a couple of days later, but he denied it and so did the boy. The next day, I was removed from the home."

"The boy?"

"Killed a year later by that same man."

"You checked on him at that age?"

Rikki shook her head. "No, but I looked into all of them when I was around sixteen."

"All of them?"

Glancing up at him, seeing his frown of confusion, Rikki whispered, "That wasn't the first time something like that happened, and it wasn't the last."

Jeremiah swore softly, running a hand gently down her hair. "How many?"

Rikki bit her lip, her eyes misting over with tears as the pain of the past engulfed her. "Fifteen. I tried to help them, but it was as if they didn't want to be helped. Except for one."

"The last one?"

"Yes," she whispered, laying her head back on his chest. "How did you know?"

"There had to be a good reason you chose to live on the streets at such a young age instead of living in a home where you were being fed and clothed."

He was right. She'd left the foster care system at the age of fifteen, running from all of the pain and betrayal associated with it. Pain she suffered through knowing what was happening to several of the kids who wouldn't speak up. Betrayal from the social workers who wouldn't look into anything further, taking the foster parent's word, along with the child's who was too terrified to come forward with the truth.

"What happened?"

Rikki's breath caught in her throat as she remembered the reason she'd decided it was better to live on the streets in the bitter cold one winter than stay in the home she'd called her own at the time. "Every time I was moved to a new home, I prayed things would be different. That whoever my foster parent was, they would have a kind soul this time, instead of a dark one. And every single time, I was disappointed. Until the last one."

Jeremiah pulled her up his body until she was lying across him and her face was buried in his neck. Stroking a hand gently over her back, he muttered, "Why do I feel like I'm gonna want to kill someone?"

Rikki slid her arms up and over his shoulders, slipping her fingers into his hair. Running her tongue slowly up the side of his neck, she bit down gently on his earlobe before snuggling close. She smiled when she heard the hiss of breath that passed his lips, loving how she made him feel.

Dragging her thoughts back to the darkness of her past, she sighed. "I was put in a home with a single woman and three other foster children. Eric was seventeen, Jimmy fourteen, and little Annie just turned twelve." Rikki smiled, remembering those days. "It was so nice, at first. Perfect. Mama Kenna was the real deal. Wonderful to all of us, treating us as if we really were her own. She helped us with our homework, encouraged us to go out for extracurricular activities, and came to every single thing we were in. Eric was a track star. I've never seen anyone so fast. Well, any human, anyway." She chuckled. "Jimmy was a true nerd. Chess club and all. Mama Kenna never missed a chess match of his. Annie loved to dance. I remember, she had a solo in her dance recital that year. I was never really any good at anything, because I was so afraid to touch something; terrified I would get a vision. Especially then. I didn't want to see something bad that would ruin the happy life I finally had. I did fumble my way through choir for a year. I couldn't carry a tune to save my life, but Mama Kenna was always there, clapping for me, her face full of pride." Rikki's voice broke, and she whispered, "I should have known it was too good to be true. Should have known it would all come crashing down around me at some point."

"What happened?"

It was a low, protective growl and Rikki smiled, tilting her head up to kiss him softly on the hard curve of his jaw. This was what she'd wanted for so long. What she craved. Jeremiah. Protective, giving a damn about what happened to her, wanting to kill anyone who hurt her. She felt loved, cherished, finally. "Mama Kenna's son moved back home after being away for four years in college. She had raised him on her own after her husband died and was so proud of him. Marty graduated top of his class in high school, earning a full ride to college with a football scholarship. He got a business degree, and had a job waiting for him when he got back. What Mama Kenna didn't know about was the darkness he hid deep down inside."

"But you knew."

Rikki nodded, her hold on him tightening. "Yes, I knew. I felt it when I met him. Something was telling me to stay far away from him. But Annie didn't feel the same. She was drawn in by his good looks and charm."

"She was twelve," Jeremiah growled, his body stiffening as if he knew what was coming next.

"Yes, she was," Rikki agreed quietly. "So young and innocent. Until he went to her room one night." A tear slipped free as she whispered, "She never told a soul. Just withdrew into herself; the pain and humiliation too much to bear."

"I want that bastard's name," Jeremiah demanded. "I don't care how long ago this was, he won't get away with what he's done."

Her heart filled with love for her big, gruff mate. Rikki ran a hand gently over his chest, trying to calm him. "It's too late," she whispered. "He's already in hell, where he belongs."

Jeremiah's hand slid into her hair, and he tilted her head up. "Tell me."

Her heart constricting, Rikki whispered, "I touched Annie's backpack one day. I saw it all. It was horrible, vile. Something that never should have happened to someone so sweet and innocent." Her eyes filling with tears, she went on, "I confronted her about it, and at first, she refused to admit it to me. Finally, a few days later, she did, and I convinced her to come forward. To tell Mama Kenna and the social worker who was assigned to her at the time."

"They didn't believe her," he guessed.

"No." Rikki's jaw tightened at the memory, angry at the injustice of it all. "The social worker thought she was seeking attention, and Mama Kenna couldn't admit to herself that her perfect baby boy may not be so perfect after all."

"They didn't even take her to the fucking doctor to have her looked at?" Jeremiah exploded, mad as hell.

Rikki shook her head, a tear slipping free. "No. Poor little Annie slipped through the cracks. Three days later, she cut her wrists in the bathroom. I was the one who found her."

"Ah, baby, I'm so sorry."

More tears streamed down her face as she whispered, "That was when I knew I couldn't stay in foster care anymore. The system was too flawed. I didn't trust it. Didn't trust anyone. So, I left. I lived on the streets for a few years. It was cold and lonely, but still better than what I'd been through before. When I was eighteen, I got my GED and then enlisted in the army. I served two years, and when I got out, I went back to the place where little Annie took her own life. To that place of misery and suffering." Holding Jeremiah's gaze, she admitted something she had never told anyone before. "I went hunting. That bastard ate one of my bullets, and I don't regret it at all. I would do it again in a heartbeat."

"Good," he growled, pressing a hard kiss on her mouth. "Good."

13

Jeremiah woke a couple of hours later, hard as a rock. Soft fingers trailed sensuously over his skin, lips kissing, sucking, tongue licking. A low groan left his throat when those fingers found his cock and began stroking him slowly. "Rikki." His beautiful mate. So strong and courageous around others, but soft and feminine with him. She was everything to him. His world.

Those lips made their way down his stomach, teeth nipping, her tongue sneaking out to soothe the small marks of pain. His dick jerked, and he dug his fingers into the bed, clutching at the sheets to stop himself from guiding her where he wanted her. She was playing, and as much as it killed him, he was going to let her.

Rikki's hand moved up over the tip of his dick, and then down again. "You're so hard, but the skin is soft," she murmured. "Like velvet."

He groaned, unable to stop himself from arching his hips and pushing into her hand. "Feels so good."

She looked up at him, a mischievous grin on her lips. "Yeah?"

"Hell yeah."

"How does this feel?"

Her tongue snuck out, wetting her lips, and then she lowered her head, licking the head of his cock. Jeremiah froze, his body alive with sensation. His dick jerked again and a shudder ran through him. Yes, she was definitely going to kill him before this was over.

"You don't know how long I've wanted your lips around my cock," he growled, watching those lips curve into a smile, before she took him into her mouth. He felt a hand on his balls, the tentative touch as she explored them. Then, she cupped them in her hand and tugged. He couldn't stop his involuntary reaction, and cursed when his hips jerked and he found himself deeper in that hot, wet mouth. "God, baby, that's so fucking good."

Tightening her mouth around him, Rikki sucked gently as she moved up and down. Her tongue stroking the tip of his dick when she raised up, and then sliding down the side as her mouth engulfed him again. It was too much, and he found himself close sooner than he wanted to be.

"Pull back," he rasped, his fingers sinking deep into her silky hair. "You gotta pull back, baby. I'm gonna come."

She growled around his cock, sending a burst of pleasure zinging through him. Her eyes glowed as she looked at him, those gorgeous pouty lips still wrapped around his length. "Mine," she snarled in warning, before swirling her tongue around the tip of his dick and swallowing him again.

His cock hardened to the point of pain at her declaration, and Jeremiah rasped, "Yours." Groaning, he gave in to the need to move, and slowly began to thrust his hips. Soon, he had to stop. It was too much. His body held taut with desire, shaking as he tried to hold back the orgasm that was already spiraling through him, he groaned, "Faster, Rikki. Harder. Suck harder." She did exactly as he wanted, and he found himself going over the edge, shouting as he came in her mouth.

Rikki swallowed all of him, licking him clean, and then slowly crawled up his body until she lay next to him, playing with the curls of hair on his chest. "I've never done that before," she admitted softly.

"Never?"

She shook her head, tugging gently on a curl. "No." She paused. "I liked it."

"I loved it," Jeremiah growled, pulling her over on top of him and guiding her hips where he wanted them. He saw her eyes widen in surprise when she felt his thick shaft nudging at her sleek, wet entrance.

"How?"

"I will never get enough of you," he growled, grasping her hips tightly. Slowly, he lowered her over his cock, gritting his teeth when he was enveloped by her heat.

"Never?"

"Never," he vowed, groaning when he was finally completely inside, pausing to make sure she adjusted to him before he began to thrust slowly inside her.

"Me neither," she whispered, before placing her palms on his chest and taking over.

"WE NEED TO GET MOVING SOON," Rikki said, placing a soft kiss on Jeremiah's chest. She'd been plastered to him all night long, waking up two more times to make love. The thought of what was coming next, what could happen when they reached Virginia, was tearing her apart. If anything happened to him, she knew she would choose to follow wherever he went. She couldn't live in this life without him. Didn't want to. "Angel will be here in an hour."

Jeremiah gently ran a hand over her back, holding her close. He didn't respond at first, just leaned down to place a soft kiss on the top of her head. Rikki fought the tears that wanted to slip free. She'd cried enough lately. She needed to be strong for her man. He was the only thing that mattered right now.

"I should have claimed you years ago," Jeremiah said, resting his cheek against the top of her head. "I'm so sorry I didn't, Rikki. I wasn't rejecting you. You were just so young. I didn't want to take your life from you. Didn't want to pressure you into a relationship with someone like me."

"Someone like you?" Rikki asked in confusion.

"Older, hard, set in my ways."

"I don't know," she murmured, skimming a hand down his chest to his abs and lower. "You don't seem that old to me. And I love the hard part."

Jeremiah grunted when her hand connected with his already thickening cock, and he grabbed it to pull it back up to his chest. "You are insatiable, woman."

"Good thing I'm yours," she said, laughter in her voice. "I need someone who can keep up with me."

Jeremiah shook his head, chuckling. "You are going to be the death of me, mate."

Rikki went quiet, her arm going around Jeremiah and holding on tightly at the thought of his death.

"I am sorry, Rikki. For not telling you about us before, for not claiming you when I should have. For not being here these past few months." Rikki froze when she heard the pain in his voice. "I thought I was doing what was right. Getting on the inside to fight the bastards who hurt you. I wanted to take down the entire organization, and I feel like the only way to do that is from deep inside. That's no excuse, though. I should have checked in. Should have called. Should have…"

Rikki placed a hand on his lips, tilting her head back to look at him. "Stop. It's enough that you're here now." And it was. She'd been so angry before, but she was beginning to understand the pull of mates more now that she had her wolf with her. With that understanding came the knowledge that she would do anything for hers. She would live for him, kill for him, die for him. How could she fault him for wanting to take care of her in whatever way he thought best when she felt the same way. Who knows what she would have done if the positions had been reversed. Probably the same damn thing.

"I hurt you," Jeremiah rasped, his eyes darkening in pain. "There is no excuse for putting your mate through what I put you through."

Rubbing her hand over his chest to try to soothe the beast she could tell was rising, she kissed his neck. "It's over and done with. We can't change the past. Neither of us can. We can only go forward."

"Together," he said gruffly.

"Together."

"Will you tell me what it was like? These past few months?"

She didn't ask him to clarify what he meant. She knew. Rikki sighed, doing the only thing she could. She told him the truth. "It was horrible. Scary, terrifying. I felt so lost and alone. The only thing that kept me going were the visits from my teammates. My family."

"You were aware the whole time?"

"Most of it, I think. It's hard to explain. There was a time when the darkness threatened to push me under and not let me back up. It was a struggle to hold on, to stay in this world. A part of me wanted to give up so badly." A low growl vibrated in his chest, and she buried her head in his neck, rubbing a hand over his skin. "I found out a few days ago that it was because one of the General's people, Ashley, had a gift where she could seep into someone's mind and make them feel things like that. Like they didn't want to live."

"What?" Jeremiah snarled, his arm tightening around her.

"Steele found her, and Chase killed her. After that, things began to get better. It was as if I were sleeping, and no matter how much I tried, I couldn't wake up. But the darkness was gone. I had the will to fight again. Doc Josie thinks it was more of a healing sleep."

"Dammit," Jeremiah growled, tugging her up until her entire body covered his. "I should have been here!"

Raising her head to look in his eyes, his gaze turbulent with emotion, she smiled. "You're here now."

"I'm never leaving you again," he vowed, his lips capturing hers.

Rikki lost herself in his kiss for a moment before pulling back to whisper, "I love you, Jeremiah Black. With all that I am. Whatever the future brings, we will face it together."

"God, baby, I love you, too." His lips found hers again, almost desperate this time. "Always. Forever."

14

"You're sure no one will be able to detect it?" Jeremiah asked, flipping down the collar of his shirt. The uniforms the guards were required to wear were all black, from the button-down short-sleeved shirt, to the cargo pants, to the shitkickers on his feet. The tiny black listening device that Jaxson had inserted under the collar in the back of the shirt was so miniscule, it would easily blend in.

"Positive," Jaxson promised, moving away and handing out ear pieces to the team. "We will be able to hear you, but you won't be able to hear us. That part sucks, but can't be helped."

"Don't worry," Trace said, patting his sniper rifle. "I got your back, man."

"Me, too," Sapphire promised, lifting her rifle in his direction.

Jeremiah's lips quirked up into a grin. "Until I get inside."

"I've seen you in action," Flame drawled. "I think you can handle yourself until we get in there."

Rikki slid in close to him, her arm slipping around his waist. "I'll be in a tree several yards away, my rifle pointed at the building the entire time."

Jeremiah heard the worry in her voice, but it was still strong, sure, determined. "I know you will," he said in a low voice. Leaning down, he captured her mouth with his, slowly tracing the plump fullness of the bottom one with his tongue. "I'll be back as soon as I can," he muttered against her lips, wishing he didn't have to leave her, but knowing there was no choice. If he didn't, everyone in that facility just ten miles down the road would die. He couldn't have that on his conscience.

The sound of the Hummer filled the air, and Jinx pulled up next to them. Putting the vehicle in park, he slid out but kept it running. "You need to hurry before they become suspicious."

"I'm sure they already are." He knew they were. He would be if it was him.

"Maybe we need to find another way," Flame said hesitantly, her gaze going from Jeremiah to Jinx. "I feel like we are throwing Jeremiah to the wolves."

"That's because we are," Angel ground out. "Unfortunately, we have no choice."

Jeremiah looked down into his mate's eyes, the dark pools of brown sucking him in. Lowering his head to kiss her gently on the forehead, he said, "There is no other way." Giving his mate one last, hard kiss, he let her go and made his way to the Hummer. Glancing back, he let his gaze roam over her, from the dark hair pulled back in a pony tail, down her small, curvy body covered in black, to the toe of her combat boots. His woman was a fighter, but she was also soft and loving, and so damn beautiful it made his heart ache.

"I love you." She mouthed the words to him, her lips turning up into a gentle smile just for him. Her hand closed into a fist, and she pressed it to her heart.

Swallowing hard, Jeremiah returned the gesture, mouthing the words back to her. His heart. His soul. His world.

JEREMIAH ENTERED the Virginia facility through a side door, using a five-digit code that was dedicated solely to him, so whoever was watching could see when he came and left each place he was assigned to. And they were watching; of that he had no doubt. They were all a paranoid bunch of bastards, as they should be. Some of the places were more lax, but not this one. It was one of the worst. Very tightly controlled by the man in charge, Lenox Keaton. You had to enter your five digits every time you went from one floor of the large three-story building to another. In the basement, you had to enter your code to enter the scientists' lab. Hell, he was surprised he didn't have to use his code every time he took a piss. He'd given that code to RARE, but had no idea how long it would work. If their suspicions were correct, his head was on the chopping block, along with most, if not all, of the people in the place. It only stood to reason they would deactivate the codes and lock them all in the building. He hoped he was wrong, but his gut told him he wasn't. He just prayed they didn't blow the thing up with him in it.

Straightening his shoulders, Jeremiah stalked down the long hallway, headed for the offices at the end. It didn't matter what they did. There were innocent people that were about to die because of Ebony. He had to do everything he could to save them, even at the risk of his own life. He gritted his teeth as a thought hit him. He and Rikki were now mated. If something happened to him, it would affect her, too. She would have to choose to live a long, lonely existence without him, or follow him into death. He knew what he would choose. It was unacceptable for her to do the same. She was important, her life was important. Which meant, he would survive. He had no choice.

Pausing in front of one of the doors, he lifted his hand and knocked.

"Enter."

Jeremiah opened the door, his gaze instantly meeting the ice-cold blue ones of the man sitting behind the desk.

"Jeremiah. Good to see you."

Bullshit. He didn't have to be a shifter to tell the bastard was lying. "Sir."

"Was there an issue with the Hummer?"

Jeremiah allowed his brow to furrow in confusion. "Issue?" Nope, no issue. Not any that wasn't caused by him, anyway.

"The tracker doesn't seem to be working."

Jeremiah shrugged. "I have no idea. Didn't even think to check." He could play Lenox Keaton's game. Lucky for him, the man wasn't a shifter and wouldn't be able to scent the lies. Not that he was technically lying. He hadn't checked to see if it was working. He'd just made sure it wasn't.

"And your phone?"

"Must have forgotten it in Arizona, sir." He'd left it. On purpose.

Keaton nodded, leaning forward to rest his forearms on the desk. "We will get you a new one."

Another lie. "Appreciate it."

"There's been a... development... since you were last here." Keaton paused. "Vixen is no longer with us. It is unclear if she is dead or a traitor. If you should see her, your orders are to take her out. Understood?"

Interesting. For some reason, they thought the assassin might return. He wondered what that meant. "Yes, sir."

Keaton raised an eyebrow. "Not even going to ask what happened?"

"No. Figured if you wanted me to know, you would tell me." Whatever the son of a bitch said would be a lie, anyway. Just one more floating around the room, and the stench was starting to get to him.

"Your things?"

"Left them in the Hummer until I had my orders."

"Bring them in. You will be staying where you did last time. Second floor, same room." Keaton pushed his chair back and rose, glancing at his watch. "Your shift starts in fifteen minutes. Got here just in time."

"Which floor am I working on?" he asked, although he had a feeling he already knew.

"Basement." Yep. They were going to keep him down below, out of whatever was taking place above. Better to keep him in the dark.

Jeremiah nodded to Keaton before turning toward the door.

"And, Jeremiah."

"Yeah?" He glanced back, stiffening slightly at the hard, calculating look on the other man's face.

"I'll be leaving tonight for a meeting. I'm taking Connors and Kozad with me. That leaves you as senior guard until we return."

Damn, that was fast. They weren't wasting any time. Which meant, he was going to have to move quickly himself. "Yes, sir. Who will be here with me?"

"A new guard, Jennings. Young kid, but good at his job. And another newbie, Rena Greyson. Been with us for a couple of months. Keep your eye on her."

"Why?"

"Kozad caught her talking to a prisoner the other day. She may be a bleeding heart."

Jeremiah scented the truth on him and nodded. "Got it."

That could work to his advantage, because it was obvious that they were getting ready to implement their plan. Jinx and Vixen had been right. Leaving a kid who was still in training behind, along with a woman they were tagging as a possible traitor to their cause, meant they were going to be collateral damage. The same as he was. Screw that.

Five minutes later, he was outside by the Hummer leaning into the backseat. "You get all that?" he asked quietly, grasping the handle of his duffle bag. He saw a small flash of light in the distance, and went on, "They are going to move quickly on this. Not sure my code will work again once I get in the basement." Another flash.

"Jennings and Rena come with us. He's young and stupid, but hopefully that stupidity is his biggest fault. Sounds like Rena could be on our side." Another flash. "If I don't make it out…" Two flashes. A small smile kicked up the corners of his mouth. "Love you, too, mate." One flash.

Shaking his head, Jeremiah backed out of the Hummer and slammed the door shut. When he went to key in his code to get back in, the door slammed open and Quinn Connors walked out. Tall and stocky, with black hair and dark green eyes that seemed to miss nothing, he was the kind of man who caught someone's eye and kept it. Quinn paused, his gaze skimming around the area before coming back to land on him. "Jeremiah Jenson. It's been a while."

"Yeah, it has." Jeremiah watched Connors closely. While Quinn had always seemed dangerous, especially because Jeremiah could feel the overwhelming power flowing from him, he'd never scented the stench of evil that wafted off most of the other guards. He'd worked with the other man once before, and had wondered just what the hell Quinn was, but he'd never been able to figure it out. A shifter, he was sure, but somehow the man managed to mask it from him. "I hear you and your lapdog are taking Keaton away from here. Leaving me alone to babysit." It was said with a sneer, because that was what was expected of him. He played the part, and he played it well.

"If that little prick, Kozad, makes it that far," Quinn grunted. "Fucker's gettin' too big for his britches. Gonna have to bring him down a peg or two."

Jeremiah chuckled. "You looking for these?" He tossed the keys to the Hummer at the man, knowing he would be giving it a thorough look-over.

"Thanks."

"See ya." Jeremiah punched his code in and opened the door.

"Not if I see you first," Quinn said, slamming a shoulder into his, cursing when he dropped the Hummer key on the ground. Leaning in, he ducked his head and muttered. "One, five, three, four, six." He squatted down to retrieve the key, and then reeled off the numbers again as he rose. Jeremiah kept his head averted and walked into the building, the door slamming shut behind him. What the hell? He repeated the numbers over and over in his mind, realizing what they had to be. Someone's personal code, like the one he had. Which could only mean one thing. Quinn Connors knew what was going to happen, and he was trying to save Jeremiah's life. The man was one of the good guys. Shit. How many of them were there in the organization that he didn't know about? Connors was in even deeper than he was, as right-hand man to Lenox Keaton. Were there more?

15

Rikki watched her mate disappear into the building in front of her through the scope of her rifle, terror filling her at the thought of him stuck in there with no way out. Ruthlessly, she shoved it down. Jeremiah needed her calm and steady, not a shaking mess. She had to be on the top of her game this mission, because the most important person in her life was in that facility, putting his life on the line. Blocking out the fear, Rikki clenched her jaw tightly and stared through the lens of the scope, never wavering.

He's going to be okay, Rikki, girl. It was Phoenix, her brother, always standing behind her no matter what. Even when she'd tried to take him down in wolf form. He still loved her. She heard it, felt it in the warmth of his voice.

Nothing can happen to him.

Nothing will, Angel said quietly. *We're here.*

What about on the inside? Rikki hated the tremor in her voice. Dammit, she had to be strong.

I got that covered.

Rikki froze at the declaration, her spine stiffening at the unfamiliar voice. No, that wasn't true. She recognized it, just never thought she would hear it in her head, on a telepathic link she and her team members shared.

Nice to see you could make it to the party, Vixen, Jinx drawled.

You better get out of here, Jinx. You need to be long gone when shit goes down.

Worry about yourself, woman.

I am. You know a lot about me now that no one else does. What if you get caught? You could give me up. I would hate to have to take you out.

Touch my son, and I will tear your heart out.

There was complete silence, and then Vixen whispered, *I wonder what it's like to have someone love you the way your family does, Jinx. There was a time when I would have given anything to find out.*

And now? Jinx asked quietly.

My life isn't one I would want to share with anyone else, Vixen admitted, and Rikki could have sworn she heard a touch of sadness in the other woman's voice. *I will always be looking over my shoulder, wondering when Ebony will send someone new after me. I wouldn't want anyone I cared about to get hurt.*

Sometimes, we don't have a choice. It was Sapphire, Steele's sister. Rikki met her for the first time out at Angel's farm just a few days ago, and she was impressed. Sapphire was a rock-solid shot. Every bit as good as Rikki, if not better. She liked her and her brother Bane, who was the complete opposite of the outgoing woman. Dark, brooding, quiet. He seemed to stay to himself.

Keep your premonitions for someone who deserves them,

Vixen murmured. *After everything I've done, I don't deserve love or happiness.*

Rikki's heart hurt for the woman. She could feel her pain through the connection, even though she was sure Vixen tried to hide it. What must it have been like to be raised by the General? To be forced to do the things Vixen and Jinx had done? To live knowing you hurt and killed, that you did horrible things required of you as the General's puppet.

Everyone should have the chance to be loved, Rikki whispered, before she could stop herself. The woman's pain was radiating through the telepathic bond, and Rikki couldn't ignore it. *You are here, helping save the innocent lives in that building, Vixen. I don't know you. To be honest, I don't trust you yet. Trust has to be earned. You are one of the General's assassins.*

Was, Vixen interjected almost absently, and Rikki got the impression that she was moving stealthily. Where was she going?

Was, she conceded.

So was I. Jinx's voice was even fainter. *Are you saying that my father and Chase shouldn't care about me after everything I've done? Cause I tried that. I got a fuck you out of it.*

Damn straight you did, Angel growled. *I don't care what you've done, Son. What you've been forced to do. You are still mine, and I will always love you.*

Same. It was Steele, his voice hard an unyielding.

No, Rikki said, her gaze narrowed on the row of windows on the first floor of the building, before going back to the door. *I was saying that even though I don't know or trust her yet, I do believe Vixen deserves to be cared for. To be loved.*

What was the code Connors gave Jeremiah? Vixen interjected, obviously intent on something else.

What? Angel asked in confusion.

The guard Jeremiah was talking to before he entered the building. He gave Jeremiah a five-digit code. I need it, but I would prefer not to violate anyone's privacy by taking it out of your head without permission.

The numbers were for you, Rikki realized, her eyes widening slightly at the knowledge, but still never leaving the scope of her rifle. *Connors is on our side?*

Yes, Vixen said simply, leaving it at that. The assassin was a contradiction, saying she didn't deserve to have anyone care about her, but she obviously cared herself. She was protective of those she considered hers to keep safe, and Connors was one of hers. She wasn't going to budge on anything else with him. Which was why she made it sound like she was alone back at Angel's place, even though she obviously wasn't.

One, five, three, four, six, Rikki whispered through the link, moving her rifle around the area in front of her, her eyes narrowing on someone as they slipped through the trees on the far side of the building. *That better be you, Vixen.*

There was a pause, and then, *It is.*

Rikki watched as Vixen, dressed all in black leather, made her way around the back of the building until she couldn't see her anymore. *What are you doing?*

Finding a place to wait near the back door. When Kozad comes out for a smoke, which he does like clockwork every day about this time, I will slip inside.

I thought the code was to get you inside?

No, that's to get us out.

Ebony's calling me. I've got to go. Good luck. Jinx's voice whispered through the link, and then he was gone.

Rikki heard Angel's small gasp, even though she knew the alpha tried to keep her agony to herself. She suffered every time her son went back into the fray. With the way Rikki was feeling right now, terrified and out of control, even though she shoved that shit down as hard as she could and concentrated on protecting her mate, she completely understood.

What if they blow the place from the inside like in D.C.? Flame asked, interrupting Rikki's chaotic thoughts.

What? Rikki gasped. *What the hell are you talking about?*

They won't, Vixen replied confidently. *Ebony is more hands on. She will send in her soldiers, and I wouldn't be surprised if she came with them. She loves the action, the high that comes with the battle.* She paused. *Not the killing so much, though.*

Bullshit, Phoenix cut in.

No, it's the truth, Vixen insisted. *The bitch isn't afraid to slit your throat if she has to, but I don't get the feeling she enjoys it. Well, unless she really hates you.*

Do you? Rikki asked, slowly scanning the area with her scope again, before going back to the door. *Do you enjoy the kill?*

Sometimes, Vixen admitted. *If it's justified.*

Justified?

I took out someone who slaughtered a family. Father, mother, two older children. They left behind a little girl three years of age. That one, I enjoyed.

Because you were that little girl, Rikki guessed, somehow knowing she was right.

No. Vixen was silent for a moment, and then said, *Not that time.*

As Rikki watched, the front door opened and a man stepped out. Short and stocky with dirty blond hair, he glanced around the area as he lit up a cigarette. *Change of plans. Your man is here, but he came out the front door.*

Got it.

Rikki waited patiently until he took his last drag, flicking it away from him, then went back to key in his code. *You're up, Vixen.*

Already there. Vixen seemed to appear out of nowhere, catching the handle of the door just before it clicked shut. She waited a second, then slipped inside after Kozad. *I'm in.*

16

Jeremiah strolled down the long hall in the basement level of the facility, with its pristine white walls, people walking around in white lab coats, and the subtle beeping noises in the background that gave the place an almost hospital feel to it. The only difference was the doctors in a hospital actually gave a shit about their patients. The scientists here were just as cold and unfeeling as the sterile environment they worked in. Here, the patients were called subjects and were shut in rooms behind thick layers of glass. Objects to be watched and studied. Just the thought of what the prisoners went through daily was enough to make him want to tear out the throat of every scientist in the place. Except for one, if she was still there.

Glancing into the rooms as he walked by, Jeremiah wasn't surprised to see most of them empty. This level was primarily for the prisoners. The guards slept on the second floor, the scientists had their rooms on the top level. They were told it gave them some separation from where they worked, but really it was just another way to keep an eye on them. With the guards' rooms on the second floor, and their base on the main level, no one went up or down the stairs without them knowing, which meant there was no one slipping out the back door and running. One of the scientists tried to leave one of the other facilities Jeremiah had worked at in the middle of the night after they couldn't handle what was going on anymore. It didn't end well for them. There were too many secrets within the walls of the facilities. Too many things the organization didn't want to get out.

Jeremiah paused outside an occupied room, his gaze on the small, slender woman inside who sat huddled in a corner, her arms wrapped tightly around her raised knees. Her head was down, the long fall of dark auburn hair covering her face. Jasmine. He'd always wondered what her name was, but had never asked. He'd tried to keep his distance as much as possible, needing to appear as if his heart was as cold as the rest of the guards'.

Jasmine raised her head slowly, as if sensing his presence. Her eyes were full of misery, covered with a sheen of tears, but she didn't cower. She bared her small teeth at him, hissing in anger. Good, she still had some fight left in her. She would need it. Resisting the urge to speak with her, to let her know that help was on the way, he turned and walked away. There were cameras everywhere, and he couldn't afford to get caught sympathizing with the enemy. Not that it would matter soon.

"Jasmine is alive," he muttered quietly, making sure he ducked his head when he walked past another camera. "I saw two new prisoners. A lynx and a wolf, both male. I…" Jeremiah paused, his eyes going to the room he'd stopped in front of. There, curled up in a little ball of fluff, was a wolf pup. Just a baby. Small, so tiny she would have fit in the palm of his hand. She turned to look at him, her dark eyes full of agony and despair. His heart broke. And then, rage hit him, harder than it ever had before. He was going to kill every fucking person in that building who had harmed this poor, sweet baby. His body trembled as he fought for control. His hands curled tightly into fists, his claws digging into his skin. A low growl built in his chest. The pup's eyes widened, and she quickly buried her face in her paws. Jeremiah realized he was scaring her, but he couldn't seem to control himself. The pup thought his aggression was toward her. Didn't understand it was at everyone else in the facility. That he would never harm her. "Rikki," he rasped, his voice low, head bowed, "I'm going to kill them all. Every last one of them." His chest heaving with the effort it took not to let his bear take over, he muttered, "They have a pup in here. Just a baby. She can't be more than a couple years old." Gritting his teeth, he growled, "They are all dead. Everyone who touched her, who hurt her. Dead."

"Jeremiah." The voice was soft, quiet, and full of concern.

He stiffened, fighting to get control over his emotions. He didn't want to hurt her. He knew she was one of the good ones. That she did everything within her power to keep the prisoners safe. She was the only scientist that he thought worthy of a free pass. But, right now, he was even questioning that.

"Dr. Wainright."

"Jeremiah, are you all right?"

His gaze went to the small pup, who was cowering

from them in the far corner of her room now, and he said the only thing he could. The truth. "No."

Anya Wainright stepped up next to him, careful to keep a small distance between them, and murmured, "They brought her in a month ago. Murdered her parents right in front of her. She's terrified, and there's not a damn thing I can do about it. If I hold her, try to make her feel better, they'll know."

He knew who 'they' were. She was talking about the guards, Lenox Keaton, and everyone above them. She would be labeled as a sympathizer and be watched even more closely than she already was. They would dig into her background, her family and friends, anything and everything they could find to see if they'd missed anything when they first hired her. They would find everything they could on her, and then make the decision as to whether or not she was a traitor. More than likely, they would find her guilty and sentence her to death. He'd seen it happen before. They couldn't afford to have their scientists become sympathizers to the prisoners, and couldn't let them leave if they did. Not that anyone who ever worked for the organization ever just left. It wasn't like a normal job. You didn't sign a non-disclosure clause when you started. If you left, you left in a body bag. "She was in her wolf form when they brought her in and hasn't shifted back since. I think she's scared and feels safer. Her wolf protects her." Leaning closer, she whispered, "She won't last long in here. It's a struggle to get her to eat or drink anything. It's as if she has no will to live."

Anya was placing her trust in him with the information she was handing over. He needed to give her something in return. "It won't be a problem much longer."

Anya was quiet for a long moment before she murmured, "Good."

"How many other prisoners are in here?" RARE would need that information, and he needed to make sure he didn't miss anyone.

"There are only four of them right now. The fox from before. They brought a wolf shifter in just after you left the last time, and there's a lynx. He's new. Only been here for a week or so." Jeremiah could tell Anya was trying to distance herself from everything, but he knew it wasn't working. He could smell the sorrow wafting off her. No matter what persona she gave off, she wasn't cold and calculating like the other scientists. She cared. He'd seen her run a gentle hand over one of the shifters out of view of the cameras before when she was taking their blood. Bending her head to talk softly to them, so soft that no one else could hear. Once, she'd even lowered her head and rubbed her cheek against Jasmine's, as if sensing she needed that close contact. He'd kept his mouth shut, knowing if anyone found out, they would kill her.

"Anya," he paused, his eyes glued to where the wolf pup was now curled around itself, facing away from the window. So small and innocent. He would free her, if it was the last thing he did. "Can I trust you?"

"Yes." Her response was immediate, her voice cool and calm. "I will give my life for any of them."

He scented the truth on her, which reinforced his decision. Slowly, he turned from the pup to walk back down the hall in the direction he'd come from, indicating with a small jerk of his head for her to follow. Stopping in front of Jasmine's cell, he said, "I need you to get word to all of them, except the pup, if you can. Ebony has placed kill orders on everyone in this facility, including me."

He heard her soft gasp. "Ebony?"

He continued walking, as if he were doing his regular routine. Several times in the past, he and the doctor had walked these halls together, chatting, so it shouldn't raise any red flags. And, if it did? Well, they were already marked for death, anyway. "The General was eliminated a few weeks ago. His daughter, Ebony, took over."

"I hate that bitch."

A short burst of laughter left his lips. He'd never heard the scientist curse before. Then, he focused on the one thing she hadn't commented on. "You knew the General was dead?"

"Yes," Anya admitted, "but that's it. They don't tell us anything down here."

"How did you know he was gone, then?"

"I have my ways."

Of course, she did. "They need to be ready to fight, to get the hell out of here when I say. I have a team coming in fast and heavy."

"When?" That was one thing he liked about the woman. She didn't ask a bunch of questions. Just the important one.

"Soon." He didn't have a set time, but he knew RARE was waiting for Keaton and his men to leave and Ebony's to attack. They'd originally thought about taking the building while Keaton was still in it, but decided it was best they wait for dark. That was when they did their best work. "And, Anya?"

"Yeah?"

"Vixen's on our side."

They had just arrived back at Jasmine's cell. Lifting a chart from a hook on the front of the door, Anya glanced over it. Then, taking out a keycard, she passed it over the small, black square by the door, grasping the handle to open it as a the tiny, almost inaudible click sounded. Her eyes going to his, she said, "I know," before disappearing into the room. He followed her, standing just inside the small area, staying near the door. It was required that a guard be with her at all times when she entered a prisoner's room. She was told it was for her safety, but they both knew the truth. It was to make sure she didn't do anything stupid. The organization didn't give a shit about her personal safety. Lucky for her, he did.

ANYA'S HEART beat wildly as she opened the door to the lynx's room twenty minutes later. She'd spoken to the fox and the wolf already, her back to the camera, her voice low, letting them know what was happening. They'd been at the facility longer than the lynx. They knew her, knew her heart and soul were good. That she didn't want to hurt them. The lynx was different. He was wild, crazy with anger. She didn't blame him. He was trapped in a small cell, which had to be hard on his cat. Add to it the tests and experiments she was required to do. Hell, it drove her crazy. She could imagine what he was going through.

She was aware of Jeremiah's presence behind her, and while it made her feel safer, she knew if the lynx went for her throat, no one would be able to stop him. For some reason, he hadn't tried to hurt her, though. She hoped today wasn't the day he changed his mind.

The large cat paced around the small area, his muscles moving under the golden fur spotted with black. He was one of the most beautiful animals she'd ever seen, and Anya had to force herself not to reach out to touch him. Anya waited patiently for him to approach her, but instead, his eyes centered on Jeremiah, and a low growl built in his throat.

"No!" she whispered, when he crouched low, as if to spring. "You can't! He's here to help."

The cat paused, his gaze going to her, his head cocked to the side as if he was listening to her.

"I need to take a sample." When he began to growl again, she whispered, "Please. I need to talk."

The great cat bared his teeth at her on a snarl.

Anya sent a quick glance to the camera in the far corner of the room. "Please."

She watched as he began to pace around the small area again, looking over at them, his lips pulling back from his fangs in another snarl. She waited, praying he would let her near.

Suddenly, he stopped a distance away from them. He stared at her, as if waiting. Anya took a deep breath and stepped in his direction. When Jeremiah put a hand on her arm to stop her, the cat growled low and deep in his throat.

"It's okay," she said quietly, pulling away from him.

"He's unstable," Jeremiah growled. "He could hurt you."

Anya looked at the lynx, her gaze going over the smooth, beautiful coat, and then back to those captivating golden eyes. "He has reason to be."

"Anya."

Anya sighed, her gaze skating around the room. "It doesn't matter, Jeremiah." And, it didn't. She would give her life if it meant the lynx lived. She owed it to him, to all of them.

"Your life means something."

"His means more." To her, it was the truth.

Slowly, she crossed the room, closing the distance between herself and the cat. Kneeling beside him, she whispered, "Please, whatever you are going to do to me, let me talk first." A shiver ran through her at the powerful growl that moved up his throat. Lowering her head, she uncapped the needle in her hand. "The man behind me can be trusted." Another deep growl that sent her heart-beat into overdrive. "He has friends close by. They are going to break in tonight and free you and the others. You need to be ready to fight." Placing the needle close to his skin, she stopped. She was so tired of hurting people. So tired of living the life she'd been living the past five years. "God, I can't do this anymore. I just can't."

"Anya. You have to. They could be watching. Listening."

Anya looked into the golden eyes that were staring back at her curiously, and she slowly shook her head. "I can't, Jeremiah. I won't hurt him anymore."

"It's a fucking needle, Anya. He will be fine."

Lifting a shaking hand, she placed it gently on the lynx's neck. He stiffened, but didn't pull away. "He doesn't like needles."

"I don't give a fuck what he likes."

Anya's fingers sank deeper into the lynx's fur, and she whispered, "I do."

"They will kill you." She knew Jeremiah said it for the benefit of the cameras. Keeping up a role he was playing. She was tired of the act. Just plain tired.

"They were going to, anyway."

"They will move up their timeline."

"Let them." Lowering her head, she whispered, "I am so sorry for everything you've been through. I hate this place. Hate the things they do. But if I have to choose between my life and yours, I choose you. I promise you, I will get you out of here tonight, or die trying." Raising her head, knowing she was on dangerous ground, she ran her hand over his neck one last time. "Thank you, lynx, for allowing me near. For letting me touch your beautiful fur. I won't forget you, even in death."

Rising, she slipped the needle into her pocket and turned to the door, her back to the lynx. If he wanted to kill her, he would do it. She was walking the tightrope of life right now, anyway, and she knew she would fall soon. Squaring her shoulders, she began to walk toward the door. She waited for an attack that never came. Soon, she was in the hallway with Jeremiah at her side. Tears filled her eyes as she glanced through the large glass window that separated her from the cat. He was staring at her, tracking her movements.

"Stand strong for just a little while longer, Anya."

"I don't know that I can," she admitted, raising a hand to rest it on the clear, cold glass. "All of the pain and suffering, it's just too much. I can't do it anymore."

"You won't have to," Jeremiah promised, his hand going to her arm to gently pull her away from the window. "Our plan has been put into motion. It won't be much longer."

Anya sighed, and after one last look at the lynx, turned to walk away. She was on borrowed time. She felt it. She may not live through the night, but the others would. The ones who were being held like animals, poked and prodded, experimented on. They would all make it, because she would accept no less.

17

Rikki waited patiently, her gaze never leaving the building or the area around it. It helped that she could hear Jeremiah's voice, even if she was unable to communicate with him. At least, she knew he was alive. Her heart had gone out to him when he found the wolf pup. She'd felt his pain and anger through their mate bond, and tried to send him love and comfort, but really had no idea how to do it, or if she even could. She wished she could reach out to him telepathically, but he didn't have any psychic abilities, and she wasn't strong enough to hold the link on her own. It would seem her big, strong bear was a softy where children were concerned, as were most shifters.

Then, she heard another woman's voice, and jealousy had slammed into her hard and fierce. She couldn't comfort her mate, but whoever Anya was, she was there with him. Right next to him. It pissed her off. Until she calmed down enough to listen to their conversation. After that, she was ashamed of herself. Anya was obviously someone Jeremiah had met before, and she could hear how much the woman was suffering. She cared about the prisoners. Was willing to put her life on the line for them. Rikki heard the love in her voice when she spoke to Jasmine, promising the fox shifter she would be free and going home to her little girl soon. Heard the fierce determination when she told the wolf that he would be back with his pack within the next couple of days. And, just now, heard the sorrow in her voice as she told the lynx she would give her life for his. Anya had guts, Rikki would give her that.

Shit, we are going to have to keep an eye on that Anya, Phoenix growled. *We don't need any fucking martyrs right now.*

Agreed. She means well, but we aren't going to let her give her life for anyone in there. Angel's voice was strong with conviction. *She lives and comes home with us.*

Ya know, you and Chase keep taking in strays like this, and you are going to have to build more apartments, Phoenix drawled.

Then, we build. What we don't do is sacrifice lives.

Agreed.

Keaton's on the move. It was Trace, who was stationed at the back of the building.

The Hummer is still out front, Rikki breathed, slowly scanning the area.

They aren't taking the Hummer. Trace paused. *Looks like they are heading through the woods.* Silence for a long moment, then, *They have an SUV back there camouflaged under some tree limbs and brush. Do I stop them, boss?*

Rikki knew all it would take was one word from Angel, and all three of the men would be eating Trace's bullets.

No, let them go. Connors is on our side, and he seems to be in deep. Since we are taking Jeremiah out, it would be nice to have an ally on the inside. Can't kill all but him. It would be too suspicious.

Roger that.

Although Rikki agreed with Angel, her finger still twitched at the thought of putting a bullet in the likes of Keaton. The bastard had left her mate to die. He didn't deserve to live himself.

You sure they won't detonate a bomb in there? Rikki couldn't help but ask the question. The thought of Jeremiah buried under all of that rock and rubble scared the hell out of her. There was no way he would survive.

Positive. The reply came from Vixen, cool and calm. *I know you have no reason to trust me, but Ebony doesn't roll like that. She may not enjoy the actual act of killing, but she loves to see the destruction caused by it. If she doesn't come here herself, she will be watching via all the camera feeds inside. She won't blow the place up.*

I really hate her.

You don't know the half of it.

Where are you at, Vixen? Angel asked, interrupting them.

Basement. Followed Jeremiah down earlier.

He doesn't know? Rikki questioned. She found it hard to believe that Vixen had followed Jeremiah into a stairwell and he didn't realize it. He was far too good for that.

Yeah, he knew. He let me.

Hate to interrupt, but we have some activity over here. Sapphire. She was on the east side of the building with her sniper rifle, scanning the area. *Assholes in black headed our way. Would be harder to see in the dark if it wasn't for the bright silver emblem on their chest. Dumbasses.*

Emblem?

Yeah, but I can't quite make it out.

I see them coming from over here, boss. So, they were coming from the back of the building where Trace was, too. Which meant they were probably going to surround the area, going in all three doors available to them.

Yep, there they were. *Got them over here, too.* It looked as if they weren't taking anything to chance. They wanted every last person in that facility dead.

Vixen, get moving, Angel ordered.

Rikki wondered in the back of her mind how Vixen felt taking orders from the RARE leader, but she heard, *Already dancing with one of the guards left behind. He's fighting hard. Not giving in.*

If you don't think he's redeemable, take him out, Angel ordered. *We don't have time to mess around. I'm sure an alarm has already been triggered somewhere.*

Got it.

Rikki, Trace, Sapphire, go!

Rikki pulled the trigger, watching in satisfaction as one of the bastards fell. Then another, and another.

Shit, there's a ton of them, Trace snarled. *They just keep coming.*

Ebony wasn't taking any chances. Keep picking them off. Everyone else, move in.

All right, you bastards, Phoenix said at Angel's order, *Let's play.*

Rikki growled, slowly moving her rifle, taking out as many of Ebony's soldiers as she could. It didn't matter how many of them Ebony sent, they weren't getting to her mate.

18

"I took out one of the guards. I'm not sure where the other one is."

Vixen. Jeremiah hadn't seen her since she followed him down the stairs earlier. "Main floor," he grunted, his Glock kicking in his hand as he pulled the trigger. The man in front of him dropped to the floor, the gun falling from his hand. Scientist his ass. If that bastard was a scientist, he would eat his own balls. The large bastard had come at him, holding the revolver like he knew how to use it.

"That bitch put some of her own men down here," he snarled. "These aren't scientists."

"Doesn't look like it," Vixen agreed, a sai appearing in her hand, and then it soared through the air until it was embedded in the throat of another threat headed their way.

He heard Anya scream, and took off at a run down the long hallway. "Get them out of their cells!" he yelled, not looking back.

He found her in her office, her hands raised as she slowly backed away from one of the male scientists. "What are you doing?" she cried.

"You are a traitor," the man said, leveling a gun on her. "I've seen how you look at those abominations. As if you care about them."

"I do care," she admitted. "They are human beings, too. They don't deserve what you are doing to them."

"They are animals. And you, are a traitor. Which is why you will die."

Not hesitating, Jeremiah raised his gun and unloaded it on the asshole. "Let's go!" They needed to get out of there quickly. Shit was hitting the fan, and they had to get topside. "Anya, now!" he hollered, trying to get her moving, but she stood staring at him in shock. When she looked around her office in confusion, he closed the distance between them, and frowned at the small circle of blood on her side that was slowly becoming larger and larger. "Shit, you've been hit."

Anya bowed her head, her hands going over the wound. When she raised her eyes to look at him, his beast growled at the resolve in them. "Go. Save them."

"Screw that," he snarled, crossing the room to pick her up in his arms.

"You can move faster without me, Jeremiah." Her breathing was becoming labored, shock kicking in. "Please, they need to come first."

"I will not sacrifice your life for theirs." Ignoring her pleas, Jeremiah cleared the office and ran down the hall to where Vixen was coming out of the wolf pup's room, the tiny furball cradled in her arms, shaking with fear. His gaze went to Jasmine, and the wolf and lynx who waited impatiently at the top of the stairs. "Jasmine, I need you to take the pup so Vixen can fight. I won't be able to since I'm carrying Anya."

"Dammit, I told you. Leave me behind. Their lives are so much more important than mine!"

"No," Jasmine said, rushing forward to take the pup from Vixen. "I wouldn't have survived here without you, Anya. None of us would have. I'm not going anywhere without you."

"You have to!" Anya argued, crying out in pain when she moved in Jeremiah's arms. "Your family needs you. I have no one. I won't be missed."

"You have us," Vixen vowed, stalking past them to the top of the stairs. "We aren't leaving you behind. End of discussion."

Tears fell down Anya's face as she glared at them stubbornly. "Then, at least let me walk. I can do that!"

Jeremiah hesitated, indecision crawling through him. He needed his hands free to fight, but he didn't trust the woman not to sacrifice herself for them. She didn't seem to see that her life mattered, too. "You sure you can?"

"Yes," she snapped, beginning to struggle in his arms. Her face went white with pain, but she smacked him in the chest. "Put me down."

Slowly, against his better judgment, he sat her on her feet. She swayed slightly, but then seemed to get her bearings. "Go," he ordered, pointing toward the stairs.

Anya began to move, slowly at first, but with determination. The lynx broke away from the others and came to walk beside her, the wolf right behind him.

"Vixen and I will go first," Jeremiah told them. "All of

you, stay right behind us. I have friends above that will be watching for us."

"They are busy taking care of the shit ton of soldiers Ebony sent," Vixen said, keying in the code in the pad next to the door. "That bitch wasn't playing around."

Jeremiah held his breath, letting it out when the door opened. Until he saw Rena standing at the top of the stairs, her gun pointed at them. Rena's gaze went past them to where Jennings lay in a heap, blood pooling around his body. "Shit." Her arm was steady, but he could scent the fear that enveloped her. "Get back down those stairs."

"Rena."

Her wild-eyed gaze on him, she shook her head. "No! Back down the stairs, now!"

"If we go down those stairs, we all die," Vixen said quietly. "Ebony wants everyone in this facility dead. That includes you."

"No." Rena shook her head in denial. "Why would she do that? You're lying!"

"Right now, she has several of her soldiers outside, trying to get in to kill what's left of us," Vixen told her. "Keaton and his men left, Rena. They are gone. We are all that are left. She wants all of us dead."

Jeremiah saw Rena's jaw harden, her eyes going cold. In that one moment, he knew she would never listen to what they had to say. Never trust them. "I don't believe you."

"Then she's already won."

"As she should."

Vixen sighed, shaking her head. "No, Rena, she shouldn't." So fast, Jeremiah almost missed the action,

Vixen slid a knife from her pants, stepped forward, and slid it across the guard's throat. He heard Anya's soft cry of alarm from behind him, but didn't turn around. There was nothing he could do for her now. He agreed with Vixen's decision to take out the imminent threat. It was her or them, and he would choose them every time.

"Which way?" he asked Vixen, knowing she was connected psychically with RARE. They would tell them the best way out.

"The front door is as good as any," she said with a shrug. "Your mate says if you get one scratch on you, she's going to go ballistic."

Jeremiah grinned, making his way down the hall to the door. "If I do, she can kiss them better later."

"I'm not telling her that."

"You afraid of my sweet wolf, Vixen?"

"Sweet is not a word I would use to describe her," Vixen said dryly, then paused. "Shit! I forgot you were wearing that damn microphone."

Chuckling, Jeremiah glanced back at her. "Chewed your ass out, didn't she? She's amazing."

Vixen glared at him, shaking her head and flipping him off. He laughed.

"Well, well, well, what do we have here?"

Jeremiah froze, his eyes going down the hall, beyond where the others stood waiting. His eyes narrowed in confusion, and he cocked his head to the side, inhaling deeply. What the fuck? "You look like Ebony, but you definitely aren't her."

The woman walked toward them, her long black hair in a high ponytail, lips painted a dark red to match the top she wore. Black leather pants covered her legs, black boots on her feet. She was a fighter, another assassin, that much was plain to see. Her eyes were cold, hard, deadly. She was there to kill them, and wouldn't stop until they all took their last breath.

"No, I'm not. Name's Envy. She's my sister, which I'm sure you've figured out. Same daddy, different mom."

"But just as evil."

The woman laughed, but it didn't reach her eyes. Eyes that were almost a pure black in color. "Call it what you want. I get the job done." Leveling her gun at the wolf, she squeezed the trigger. A deep growl left the wolf's throat, and then a quiet whine, as he collapsed to the floor in pain.

"No!" Anya cried, dropping to her knees beside him, holding her hands to his wound to try to stop the bleeding.

"Seems to me you should be worrying about your own problems instead of his," Envy said, grinning darkly, motioning to Anya's side. "Maybe you can bleed out together."

Anya glared at her. "Go to hell."

"Been there, done that, got the tee shirt." A low growl filled the hallway, and the lynx bared his huge fangs at her. "Awe, such a pretty kitty. Wonder how you will look dead and stuffed on my wall?"

Anya moved in front of the lynx quickly when the woman pointed her gun in his direction. "Enough!"

Grinning, Envy tilted her head to the side. "Are you willing to die for an animal?"

"He's not an animal."

"Seriously? Look at him? He's a fucking cat."

"He's also a human being!"

"I'll ask you one more time. Are you willing to die for him?"

Anya didn't hesitate. "Yes."

"No!" Jeremiah roared, springing forward at the same time the lynx slipped past Anya. Neither of them were fast enough. Ebony's sister pulled the trigger, her mouth twisted up in an evil grin.

<hr>

RIKKI HEARD her mate's loud roar, felt his rage, and then heard the loud pop of a gun firing... twice. Her hand on her rifle, she took out two more soldiers before grabbing hold of a tree branch and swinging down, dropping to the ground. She knew Jeremiah and the others were in the front of the building, so she ran to the side door hoping to sneak up behind them. Skirting around the fighting, she leaped over dead bodies that littered the ground. She flinched when there was the loud screeching snarl of a lynx in her ear, and then Jeremiah's voice, low and deadly. "You are a dead woman."

"We all have to die sometime."

Rikki keyed in the code she remembered from Connors and slipped into the side of the building. It took her a moment, making her way down two wrong hall-ways, before she found them. The lynx stood over a woman who was bleeding out all over the floor, her long mass of hair tangled around her, her eyes staring unseeing down the hall in Rikki's direction. There was blood drip-ping from the lynx's front shoulder, but he didn't let it stop him. A wolf lay next to them, his breathing labored as he fought for his life. Vixen stood, legs apart, a sai in each hand, her eyes never leaving the woman in front of her who held her gun on them. Another woman, smaller than the rest, held something close to her as she seemed to try to fade into the walls behind her.

"You were sent by Ebony? She must have known her soldiers wouldn't make it through." Rikki saw Jeremiah move slightly, as if to try to cover Anya more.

The woman, Envy, shrugged. "She didn't have to send me. When I heard what she had planned, I volunteered to come. Sounded like fun."

"You think killing people is fun?"

"Yes, actually, I do."

Rikki dropped to a knee, lifting her rifle and sighting it in. Her wolf was pushing at her, trying to get out to protect their mate, but Rikki struggled to stay calm. She had no control over her wolf when she set her free, but this she could control. This was something she had done for years. Something she was good at. She would protect her mate in the way she knew how.

"You are one sick bitch," Vixen said, slowly beginning to twirl one of the sais.

Envy laughed. "You mean you don't get excited whenever you pull the trigger, or when you cut someone with one of those things?"

"No, I don't."

"I do," Rikki called out, waiting until Envy swung around to stare at her in surprise before she pulled the trigger. The bullet lodged between her eyes, eyes opened wide in shock, and she slowly collapsed to the ground, her gun held tightly in her hand.

Rikki heard a loud commotion behind her, but she didn't turn around. Her nostrils flared, and the scents of her teammates washed over her. Her eyes didn't leave her mate's. He stepped away from the carnage behind him, his gaze on her, his arms opening wide. She was down the hall and launching herself at him in seconds, his name on her lips as she held him tightly.

Vaguely, Rikki was aware of Nico rushing past her to where the wolf and Anya lay, Jaxson, Bane, and Sapphire on his heels. Lost in her mate, she didn't get jerked back to the present until she heard one of them say they were losing her. Anya.

"Shit."

Rikki heard the pain in Jeremiah's voice, and she held him tightly to her as they watched Nico and Jaxson work on Anya while Bane and Sapphire tried to save the wolf.

"I got the bullet out of him," Bane said, holding a hand out to his sister. "Need to stitch him up."

"Got the one out of her side, but the one in her chest is lodged in deep. I'm going to prep her as much as I can, but we need to get her back to Doc Josie for surgery, now."

Rikki gasped when the lynx who stood guard over Anya shifted, and a dark haired, golden skinned man took his place. Ignoring his own injury, he looked at Nico. "Is she going to make it?" he asked gruffly, reaching over to run a hand down her hair.

Nico wiped at his brow, shaking his head. "I honestly don't know."

"She saved my life. Took a bullet that was meant for me." Rikki heard the confusion in the male's voice.

"Because she cares," Jasmine said, stepping forward.

"She doesn't even know me," he argued, his hand stroking her hair once again.

"She cares about all of us," Jasmine insisted, clutching the small pup in her arms. "You have to save her. Please."

"I'll do my best," Nico promised.

"That isn't good enough," the man growled, his fingers sliding gently over Anya's cheek.

"Who is she to you?" Angel asked quietly, but Rikki was sure she already knew.

"Mine," the man growled, lowering his head to rub his cheek against Anya's. "She's mine."

EBONY STARED DISPASSIONATELY at the feed that played across the screen in front of her. She'd just watched one of her sisters get shot in the head, a sister who actually had something going for her, and it pissed her off. Another thing that had her shaking with unsuppressed rage was watching how disloyal her employees were. Well, her father's employees. She would pick them better in the future. But all of this did raise a question.

"Jinx."

"Yeah?" He was standing behind her, close to the door. She didn't trust him, never had, but he was the best at what he did. She needed him. She was just going to have to figure out how to keep him on a tight leash. Her father had never been good at that. It needed to change.

"How the hell did they find out about what was going to happen at the facility in Virginia?"

"No idea."

"None?"

"No."

Ebony nodded slowly, her eyes still on the screen in front of her. "I thought you said Vixen was dead?"

"No, I said she failed."

It was the truth. But, in his line of work, to fail meant one was dead, because the assassins didn't keep anyone alive. Ebony stayed quiet for now. She didn't believe him, but she had more important things to worry about. She had a meeting to attend. At Gavin's penthouse.

19

"I have to go," Jeremiah said quietly, moving his chair closer to Rikki's and sliding an arm over her shoulders. "I went dark, Rikki, with no warning. I need to go back and be debriefed. There are going to be lots of questions, a lot of meetings, and chances are good I'll be without a job when I get back."

"That would be good for me," Chase said, from where he sat behind his large, cherrywood desk. "I could use another good enforcer on my team." He paused. "Unless, you are thinking about joining RARE?"

Jeremiah ran a hand down Rikki's arm, leaning over to kiss the top of her head gently. He could feel the tension in her, knew she was upset, but there wasn't anything he could do about it. He worked for the Federal Bureau of Investigation, and when you did something like he did, there were bound to be consequences. "Naw, I'll leave RARE to the pros."

Rikki glanced up at him, an eyebrow raised. "The pros? You probably have more experience than I do."

Dropping a kiss to her lips, he grinned. "Yeah, but could you imagine how I would react on a mission with you. I'm too overprotective. I would want to kill anyone who looked at you wrong."

Rikki shrugged. "If I'm on a mission, then chances are they are going to die anyway."

Jeremiah laughed. That was his Rikki. Stronger than most people he knew, and not afraid to tell it like it was. "True." Glancing over at Chase, he nodded. "Thank you, Alpha. I will consider your offer and talk it over with Rikki."

"I would want you on my elite team," Chase told him. "Which means, when we get missions from the council, you go with us."

"What?" Rikki asked in confusion. "What elite team? Missions from the council?"

"Chase has his own team similar to RARE," Angel explained, laughter in her eyes. "They work for the council."

"Are you shitting me?"

Angel burst into laughter, shaking her head. "No. I didn't know about it until just recently myself."

"Wow. I really missed out on a lot, didn't I?"

Angel's eyes turned gentle, and she nodded. "Yes, you did. But don't worry. We will get you all caught up while your mate is gone."

"How's the wolf pup?" Jeremiah asked, when he saw the sadness begin to creep back into Rikki's dark eyes.

"She's going to be just fine. We were able to track down her mother's side of the family. Little Sammie's aunt is taking her in."

"Thank God," Rikki whispered. "The thought of her being without anyone. It's just wrong."

Jeremiah tightened his hold around her shoulders, knowing she was remembering her own past. Rubbing the smooth skin on her arm with his thumb, he kissed her temple gently before turning back to Chase and Angel. "And Jasmine?"

Angel's eyes lit up, a wide grin spreading across her face. "Jasmine is home with her family. Vixen and I took her yesterday, and you should have seen how happy she was to hold her little girl again." A shadow passed over her face, but then it was gone again. "It won't be an easy road after everything she's been through, but she's strong. She'll make it, with the help of her mate and family."

"And Anya?"

Angel's hand covered Chase's shoulder, and she let him speak this time.

"Anya is going to make it. It's going to be a hard struggle, but she's a fighter."

"I worry about her," Jeremiah admitted with a sigh. "She's a good person, but she has no one. No one to help her through this, to fight with her."

"Not true," Rikki said, looking over at him, her eyes full of compassion. "She has us."

"That she does, little mate," Jeremiah said gruffly, pulling her closer. "That she does."

"She also has her mate."

Jeremiah's eyes narrowed. "Anyone vet him out, yet?"

Chase grinned, nodding. "You bet your ass I did. He passed."

"Good. That's good." Jeremiah was glad. Anya was going to need people in her corner.

RIKKI SAT by Anya's hospital bed, watching the woman closely. Her eyes fluttered, then fluttered again, before they finally opened. She found herself staring into startling blue eyes, the color of the bluest ocean.

"Hey," Rikki said softly, reaching over to cover the woman's hand with her own. "How are you feeling?"

Anya's lips parted, and those clear blue eyes slid shut again.

"Oh, no you don't, lady. I think you've slept more than enough already, don't you? Come on. It's time to wake up and live again."

Anya moaned, licking her dry lips.

"Thirsty? Yeah, that's one of the worst things about sleeping your life away. You are always so damn thirsty." Grabbing the large cup full of ice and water next to the bed, Rikki moved in close. Positioning the straw near Anya's lips, she said, "Here you go. Drink, but not too much at first. It won't go down as easily as you think until after a few swallows."

Anya's eyes fluttered open again, and she frowned in confusion, but she leaned over and took small sips of the water.

"Wondering how I know all of this?" Rikki asked, placing the cup back on the table and smiling at the woman.

Anya nodded slowly, her tongue slipping out to wet her lips. "Yes." It was a hoarse whisper, and Rikki saw Anya wince in pain.

Smiling encouragingly, Rikki told her, "Don't worry.

That uncomfortable feeling in your throat won't last long, either. I promise."

"Who are you?" Anya rasped, her brow furrowing.

"I'm Jeremiah's mate," Rikki said, reaching over to gently push a piece of long, brown hair away from Anya's cheek. When her eyes widened, Rikki grinned. "Didn't know that he was a shifter, or didn't know he had a mate?"

"Neither," Anya admitted quietly.

Rikki leaned back in her chair, crossing one leg over the other and folding her arms over her chest. "Well, how about I tell you a story, then?"

"Story?"

"Yeah, about a bear and his wolf." Rikki smiled when she saw a spark of interest in Anya's eyes. "Before I begin, Anya, I want you to know something. You *will* get through this. It's going to be a tough road, it's going to take some time, but you will survive."

Anya's eyes misted over, and she whispered, "I feel so alone."

"I get that, but you need to understand that you aren't alone. I'm here, Jeremiah will be back soon. There's a wolf next door who wants to meet you. And there's a lynx who has hardly left your side since you saved his life."

"What?"

Rikki nodded over to where the lynx lay curled up on the floor in the corner. "His name is Teagan Lenthrope. He's from California. That's where they first caught him."

"What? They told me my facility was the first one he'd been to."

"Not true," Rikki told her gently. "Yours was the

fourth, and since they couldn't break him, it was meant to be the last."

"Oh, my God!" As Anya looked at the lynx, tears slipped out, sliding down her face. "No wonder he won't shift. He probably feels safer as a lynx. More deadly."

"Trust me," Rikki said with a chuckle, "Teagan is deadly in any form."

Anya held out an arm to the cat, whispering, "I want to touch you. Please. I need to."

Teagan rose slowly, stretching his legs out one at a time. He stalked around the room for a moment, before stopping next to the bed. Rising on his hind legs, he shoved his head into Anya's hand, purring when she began to stroke his ears.

Anya smiled, a sparkle coming back onto those blue eyes. "You are so beautiful."

The cat purred loudly, and then it was gone, and the man was in its place. Anya gasped, her eyes widening. Her hand fell to the blankets, and then she lifted it back up to touch Teagan's cheek. "Hello."

"Hey," he said gruffly.

"I know you." Anya captured one of his hands with hers. "How do I know you?"

"You are mine," he said simply, covering the hand on his cheek with his own, and turning to place a kiss in the palm.

"Yours?"

"My mate."

"Mate?" Tears streamed down her face as she shook her head. "How could you want me after everything I've done?"

"We will work through all of that," Teagan promised,

rubbing the back of her hand over his cheek. "Right now, rest. Listen to Rikki's story."

"Don't go!"

"I won't be far, sweet Anya," Teagan promised, leaning down to brush his lips over the top of her head. Then he was his cat again, purring into Anya's hand, before dropping from the bed and making his way back to the corner to curl up, watching from afar.

Rikki smiled, knowing it was going to take time for the two of them to work things out, but the mate bond was a powerful thing. She knew they would work through everything, and they would be stronger for it.

"So," she began, as she picked the water cup up to give Anya another drink, "back to this bear and his wolf."

20

"Concentrate, Rikki."

"I can't do this," Rikki snapped, standing in the middle of the barn in her underwear and nothing else. Sweat poured over her as she fought to keep her wolf contained. She was terrified that if she let her out again, she would try to kill someone this time.

"Call to your wolf," Angel encouraged gently. "She's right there waiting. I can feel her."

"What if she tries to hurt someone again, Angel? With Jeremiah gone still, I'm afraid I won't be able to control her."

"You talk to Jeremiah almost every day," Angel reminded her. "He's fine and will be home soon. You know it, your wolf knows it. It's been too long, Rikki. You need to let her out."

"Where's Chase?"

"He's right outside."

"He should be in here with me, dammit! He's my alpha, and he should be here helping me."

Angel paused, cocking an eyebrow. "You've accepted Chase as your alpha?"

"Well, yes."

"Has your wolf?"

"Yes."

"When did this happen?"

"When he almost kicked my ass when Cujo went crazy on everyone last time. It took a little while for it to sink in, but she must have finally decided that he is stronger than she is."

"I think it is more that she realized he would protect you at all costs. I'll be right back." Angel left, but was back soon with Chase. "Okay, we are both here. Now, let her out, Rikki. I promise, it will be okay."

Rikki groaned, her body vibrating in excitement and fear, then she closed her eyes and called to her wolf. She was there instantly, a soft brush against her skin, a rumble in her throat. Rikki felt her muscles begin to stretch, bones pop, but this time instead of fighting it, she merged fully with her wolf, instinctively knowing it would be better not to fight it. It took a few minutes, but finally she was standing in front of Chase and Angel on four paws, craning her head to look up at them.

Chase smiled, kneeling beside her. "How are you feeling, little wolf?"

Rikki cocked her head to the side. She was surprised to find out that the rage and anger inside her were gone. Without them, she felt... good. Great. When Chase ran a hand gently over her fur, Rikki leaned into him with a sigh. The feelings of trust and belonging that hadn't been there before were out full force now. She trusted the man running his fingers through her fur. Knew he would watch over her, protect her from all else. There was a bond between them, different from the one that connected her to her mate, but it was there. She could feel it. And there were others. Pack. Lifting her head, she howled loudly. Chase chuckled, patting her neck before standing. When he rose and stepped away, she howled again. Then, she paused when a scent drifted into the barn, tickling her nose. Not just any scent... the scent of her mate.

Rikki raced to the door, scratching at it and whining until Angel opened it with a laugh. She knew she could have shifted and gone to meet Jeremiah, but her wolf wanted to play, and so did she. She paused right outside the barn, her eyes on the man who stood just a few yards away. Damn, he was gorgeous. He was talking to Nico and Phoenix, but she knew the second he realized she was there. He turned to her and grinned. Jeremiah held out a hand, but she shook her head. When his eyes narrowed, she threw her head back and howled loudly, almost as if in challenge. Then, she turned and ran.

JEREMIAH STRIPPED QUICKLY, ignoring the jeering calls of the others. If his wolf wanted him to chase her, he was going to chase her. The thought of what he was going to do when he caught her had him leaping forward, shifting in midair. He heard someone mutter, "Holy shit!" as he came down on all four large paws, but he ignored them. The only thing on his mind now was his mate. The hunt was on.

Rikki was fast, and it took Jeremiah a good twenty

minutes before he finally caught up with her. He lumbered through the forest behind Angel's farm, lifting his head and inhaling deeply. Her sweet scent poured into him, and a low rumble started in his chest. She was so close he could fucking taste it. He wanted her, had missed her so much. Needed to be balls deep inside her.

It was by chance that he saw her tail rising up behind a fallen log, and then he saw her peeking over the top of it mischievously. He growled in warning, a warning she didn't heed. She was off like a streak of lightning, with him right behind her. They played like that for another fifteen minutes or so, but then he'd had enough. He couldn't wait any longer. When she stood less than twenty feet away from him, dancing around lightly on her feet, Jeremiah shifted. "Baby, your wolf is so beautiful, but I need you now. Please, come back to me. I've missed you so fucking much."

As he watched, the wolf paused, cocking her head to the side, and then Rikki stood where the wolf had been. "I missed you, too," she breathed.

Jeremiah quickly closed the distance between them, sinking his hands into the thick strands of her hair. Tilting her head back, he covered her mouth with his. He deepened the kiss when she moaned, sliding his tongue inside her mouth and tangling it with hers. Holding her still, he ravaged her mouth, taking all she was willing to give.

Rikki pressed her body against his, scraping her nails down his back. Jeremiah groaned, shuddering at the small bite of pain. Pulling back, he nipped at her lips hungrily, stroking over them with his tongue afterwards. "Rikki," he groaned against her mouth. "I don't think I can be gentle."

"Did I ask you to be?" she snarled, raking her nails down his back again, this time running them all the way down over his ass. "I want you, Jeremiah. Deep inside me, where you belong. I need to feel you. Now."

"I fucking love you," he growled, sliding his hands below the curve of her ass to lift her in the air. Turning, he placed her back against the tree trunk next to him. "Tell me if it hurts."

"Just get inside of me."

He grinned at her order, then shifted her higher, sliding the tip of his cock into her wet heat. He paused, a shudder running through him as the walls of her hot sheath tightened around him. "You feel so good," he rasped. "So tight. Hot. Mine."

"Jeremiah!" Rikki wrapped her legs around his waist, her hands going to his shoulders, nails digging in as she held on. "Show me!"

"What?" He loved the little moans that slid out of her as he began to move, a slow deep thrust, and then back out.

"Show me that I'm yours," she demanded.

Her deep brown eyes began to glow with a slight golden tint, and the tips of her fangs showed past her lips. It drove him wild.

"You are mine," he snarled, grasping her hips tightly as he pushed into her. "Now. Forever. Always."

"Yes!" Rikki cried, her eyes going to his shoulder where her mate mark was as he began to pound into her. "Yours!"

Letting his fangs drop, Jeremiah lowered his head to her shoulder, licking at his own mate mark.

"Please, Jeremiah!"

He didn't make her wait. Opening his mouth wide, he sank his fangs in deep, groaning when he felt her shatter around him. So fucking hot and wet, and all his. Then, her teeth were in him, and he let out a roar as he lost control, spilling inside her.

Jeremiah rode out his orgasm, holding his mate close, his teeth still deep in her skin. He needed this so badly. The last couple of weeks without her had been hell. That was the last time he was leaving her for any long length of time. It was too much for him, too much for his bear.

"I love you, Jeremiah." Her words were a soft whisper against his skin, as she licked over the mating bite. "So much."

Slowly, reluctantly, he removed his fangs and ran his tongue over her soft skin to help the bite heal faster. "I love you, too, little wolf."

Rikki hesitated before asking, "Do you have to go back?"

"No, baby," he said quietly, slipping out of her and lowering her down on her feet. Gently, he wiped the small pieces of bark from her back. "My time with the bureau is over. I'm here for good."

"Is it wrong that I'm happy about that?"

"Why would it be?" he asked, looking down at her in surprise. "I am."

Rikki shrugged, ducking her head shyly. "We never really talked about what we were going to do. Where we would live. I know you have a life where you were before. Family, friends. I don't want to take you away from everyone and everything you know."

Jeremiah cupped her face in his hands, tilting her head

up until he was looking into her beautiful, expressive eyes. "You are all that I need, Rikki Diamond."

"But your family? Family is important."

"Yes, they are, but mine doesn't live near me. My family is large and spread out all over the United States. Trust me, they don't care where I live as long as I visit sometimes. As for friends," he shrugged, "I never had time to make any close friends. My work was my life. Now, you are."

Rikki watched him closely, as if gauging the truth of his words, and then a large grin spread across her face. "You're mine, too, Jeremiah."

Sliding an arm around her waist, Jeremiah tugged on her to get her moving, and they started to make their way back toward the farm. "I thought I might talk to Chase about that job offer he had."

"Yeah?"

"Yeah. I'd like to be out there helping people again, Rikki. Being behind a desk, that's not me."

"No," she agreed, smiling up at him. "It's not."

Jeremiah stopped walking, his full attention on the woman who was looking at him with pure love shining in her eyes. "You are my everything, Rikki. I hope you can deal with that. I will try not to be too overly protective, but it's in my nature. I'm not sure how much I can hold back."

Rikki placed a hand on his chest, then leaned up and nipped at his chin. "I want to be your everything."

Jeremiah growled, covering her lips with his. Soon, he was lowering her to the ground and slipping back inside her. Moving slowly, making love, showing her what she meant to him.

21

Rikki was surprised to see Jinx at the farm when they returned. She slipped back into the barn in her wolf form, shifting quickly and putting her clothes on. She was back moments later, sliding under her mate's arm, a slight blush of color on her cheeks. They would all know what she and Jeremiah had been doing. Would be able to smell it on them. She didn't care. The man at her side was hers. That's all that mattered.

"Rikki, Jinx is actually here to see you." When she glanced over at Angel in surprise, she said, "He brought something of Amber's with him. He's hoping you can use your gift to figure out where she might be."

Amber. The General's daughter. According to everyone, she was good, kind, and sweet. Everything his other daughters weren't. Rikki found that hard to believe, but if it was true, if Amber had done all of the things she'd done for the people Rikki cared about out of the kindness of her heart, then she deserved to be rescued. You couldn't help what family you were born into, and if Amber was the saint everyone made her out to be, Rikki couldn't imagine the hell she was going through right now.

Stiffening, Rikki clasped her gloved hands tightly together in front of her before nodding slowly. "I can try." She hadn't tried to read anything since she woke from her five-month beauty nap, and really didn't want to now. Her ability was unpredictable. She never knew where it was going to take her, but she would do this for the woman who had helped so many others.

"We need to wait for Bane. He should be here soon."

"Bane?"

"She's his mate," Angel said softly.

Rikki's eyes widened, and suddenly, what she was about to do seemed that much more daunting. She knew what it was like, having her mate out there somewhere, not knowing where. Not knowing if he was alive or dead. If he was in pain or suffering. She had gone through that hell herself and didn't wish it on anyone. "I didn't know."

"He's not taking it well," Angel admitted, her gaze going to the road. A large pickup was making its way toward them at a high, almost reckless speed. "He's stuck between accepting her as his, and wishing she wasn't because of who she is."

"She can't help that," Rikki argued, moving closer to her mate.

"I agree, but that doesn't make it any easier on Bane."

Rikki nodded, leaning her head against Jeremiah's shoulder. Hadn't she just been thinking along those same lines? That she didn't know how she could trust someone related to that bastard, the General? Why did finding out Amber belonged to Bane make things different? She didn't know for sure, but it did.

"I think you will find things have changed, somewhat," Jinx said, leaning up against the side of a small, all black, sleek two-door car. Was that a Porsche? Where the hell did Jinx get his toys?

"In what way?" Angel asked, as the truck came to a screeching halt a few feet from them. Bane jumped out of the driver's seat, stalking toward them, his face in a dark and dangerous scowl.

"He knows he can't run from the inevitable."

"I told you to stay the fuck out of my head, nephew," Bane growled, glaring at him.

Jinx just grinned. "About time you woke the hell up."

"Let's do this," Sapphire interrupted. "I've been getting flashes of something over the past couple of days. I'm not sure what's going on, but I think it's Amber, and I think she's in trouble."

"Flashes?" Rikki asked in confusion. Angel had filled her in on a lot that had gone on over the past few months, but it was obvious she'd left a few things out. There'd been so much, Rikki didn't blame her.

"Visions," Sapphire told her. "Normally, I see more clearly in them, but this one is blurry. Fuzzy. I don't know how to explain it."

"Maybe Amber's future isn't destined just yet?" Angel suggested. "Futures can alter, change, with each new development in life."

"True."

"I'm ready," Rikki told them, removing her gloves and handing them to Jeremiah.

"Do you need anything from me?" he asked, encircling her waist with his arm and pulling her close protectively.

"Just what you are doing." Rikki smiled up at him,

tilting her head up for his kiss, before looking back at Jinx. Holding out her hand, she waited while he unwrapped a small wooden carving of a wolf painted black, his eyes a deep brown. He was standing proudly on all fours, his nose pointed in the air, mouth open in a silent howl.

"Wow," Angel whispered, reaching for it, but stopping right before she touched it. Rikki knew it was for her benefit. The more people who handled the wolf, the harder it would be for her to catch a vision. Jinx seemed to understand that, too, because he only allowed the piece of cloth he held to touch it, nothing else. "It's magnificent."

"Amber made it," Jinx told them, holding it up for them to see. Turning it over, he showed them the small patch of white on its stomach, and the white circle on the pad of one paw.

"It's my brother," Sapphire breathed in awe, taking a step closer. When she reached out to touch the wolf, Jinx swiftly pulled it back.

"Yes," Jinx agreed. "It's Bane. Only Amber has worked with this wood. It's had no other touch except hers. Her energy is surrounding it. It's best it stays that way for now, until Rikki does her thing. Too many different energy vibes will throw her off."

"How did you know?" Bane's tone was hard, but Rikki heard the pain underneath it, felt the man's agony he tried to hide from everyone.

"Let's just say, Amber has a few gifts herself."

"She kept them hidden from the General, didn't she?"

Jinx nodded to Angel. "For the most part. She

pretended to be less than she was, so she would be in a better position to help those in need."

A low growl built in Bane's throat. "My mate is not less than anyone."

A slow grin spread across Jinx's face, and he nodded. "Glad that you can finally see that, Uncle." Bane's eyes narrowed on him, but he didn't respond.

"Give it to me," Rikki said, pulling from Jeremiah's arms. It felt as if something were pushing her. The small wolf figure was beckoning, the energy around it pulsing, calling to her. Jinx held it out, and her fingers closed around it, clutching it tightly in her hand.

Immediately, she was swamped with several different emotions that brought her to her knees. Rikki heard Sapphire cry out, but she ignored her, concentrating on the emotions. Pain, sorrow, helplessness, guilt, fear. It was so much, almost too much. Crippling. She felt strong arms engulf her from behind, holding her against a wide chest, and breathed in the scent of her mate. It calmed her. Steadied her. Made it so she could stay connected to whatever was happening and continue down the path it was taking her.

THERE WAS a small flash of pain, and then she was in a place that was similar to a dungeon. It was as if she were watching from above, staring down in horror at the scene below her. A young girl, no more than ten, with long, blonde hair that touched her waist, and large brown eyes with a hint of gold stood beside a man who looked as if he'd been beaten almost to death. He was growling at her, his large teeth threatening to bite into her. She *flinched, but stood stubbornly in front of him. As Rikki watched, the girl moved closer, holding out a piece of bread. The man grabbed her wrist, and the child cried out in pain, but didn't fight.*

"Please, eat. I brought some water, too." As the man stared at her in confusion, she reached out and touched his arm lightly. "I would get you out of here if I could. Someday, I will be strong enough to free you. To free all of you."

The man watched her closely, then slowly released her. He sniffed the bread carefully before taking a bite, then devoured it as if he hadn't eaten in days. When the girl gave him the bottle of water, he downed it quickly.

"I have to go now, but I promise, I'll be back."

The man watched her go, his eyes narrowed on her until she was out of sight.

IT WAS AMBER AS A CHILD, there was no doubt in Rikki's mind. She'd never seen her before, but Angel had described the woman to her. The long blonde hair, wide eyes… it was definitely Amber. Suddenly, the vision changed.

THE GIRL WAS OLDER NOW. Maybe sixteen or seventeen. She stood in front of the General, her head held high, streaks of blood covering every inch of her body that Rikki could see. She had to be in pain, but she never took her gaze from the General.

"You defied me, daughter. Because of that, you were punished."

"Yes, sir."

"Do not fail me again."

"Yes, sir."

"They are animals. Abominations. Nothing more. Do you understand? You will stay away from them, or you will suffer the same fate they do."

"Yes, sir."

RIKKI COULDN'T IMAGINE the will power it took to stare that bastard in the eyes, never flinching when he looked at her with that cold, unfeeling gaze. He had ordered someone to whip her. Who did that to his own child? "Amber." The woman's name was a breath on Rikki's lips. She didn't realize how that one word radiated with anguish to the people surrounding her as she was sucked into another vision.

"No, I won't go. They will kill you if they find out what you've done for me."

"Then I will die for a worthy cause." Amber opened a door, motioning to the woman behind her. *"Come on, Gemma. We have to hurry."*

They ran from the room, down a long hallway to a side door. Amber keyed in a code, then slipped through it, waiting for Gemma to follow. Soon, they were out in the middle of the woods. It was dark and cold, a light dusting of snow on the ground.

"Amber, come with me. Please. My pack will protect you."

Amber glanced over at Gemma with a sad smile. "No one can protect me from him, Gemma."

"We can," Gemma said stubbornly.

Amber hugged the woman tightly, then leaned back and touched her cheek lightly. "Follow this path for the next mile. It will take you to a river where I've hidden a small row boat. I've sent a message to your pack. Someone should meet you a few miles down the river."

"Amber." Gemma's eyes filled with tears as she wrapped her arms around Amber tightly, holding her close. "I don't know what I would have done without you, my friend. Please, stay safe."

"You, too."

Amber watched Gemma leave, her shoulders slumping slightly when she turned to head back down the path.

RIKKI WATCHED several more images similar to the ones she'd already seen. Images of the past, proving how giving Amber was. How she put her life on the line daily to try and protect all of the people whose lives the General ruined. She couldn't imagine having the courage to go through the things Amber did, and still press forward. Still put your life on the line for others. There was a goodness in the woman that Rikki had never seen. Then, the visions changed.

A WOMAN LAY ON A COT, her gaze unseeing. Her once long, blonde hair was now tangled and ragged. Her eyes that were a beautiful brown, now dull and glazed over, as if she had finally broke and was hidden somewhere deep inside herself. Dressed in what looked like a hospital gown, she was thin, almost boney. She shivered uncontrollably in the cold room.

The door opened, and Amber flinched slightly, the only indication Rikki had seen so far that she was still lucid.

"Your sister sends her greetings," a man said as he walked in

carrying a tray. "*She's unable to make it to see you right now, but soon. She hopes you are enjoying your time here.*"

Rikki saw a glint of something in Amber's eyes, and then it was gone. When the man left, Amber turned on her side facing the wall. Slowly, she started talking, and Rikki was shocked to find out she was talking to her.

"*I know you are here. I can feel you. I don't know who you are, but please, help me.*"

Rikki froze. Then she tried to respond. "Can you hear me?" She had never done anything like this with her gift before. It didn't work this way. She couldn't talk to people in her visions, only see what was happening. And, while she could use telepathy, she wasn't strong enough to hold a connection like this.

"*Yes.*"

Holy shit! It had to be Amber connecting with her. There was no other explanation. "Amber, my name is Rikki. I'm with RARE."

"*Rikki? I don't know you.*"

"That makes two of us." When she felt the vision beginning to fade, she growled, "Amber! You need to tell me where you are."

"*Florida,*" *came the soft reply, as Amber's eyes began to drift shut.* "*So tired.*"

"What part of Florida?" When there was no response, Rikki hollered, "Don't you dare pass out on me, Amber! Where in Florida?"

"*Don't know.*"

"We are going to find you, Amber."

"*Cold.*"

"Amber! We are coming. Your mate is coming."

A small frown appeared, but Amber's eyes didn't open.

"Mate. Wolf. So beautiful." The words were a soft whisper, one
Rikki almost missed, then she was gone.

RIKKI WAS YANKED from the vision and found herself
screaming Amber's name. "It's okay," Jeremiah said soothingly, rubbing his hands over her arms. "You're back from
wherever the hell you were. Safe."

Rikki looked up at him with tear-filled eyes. "But
Amber's not."

"Tell me," Angel demanded, ignoring Jeremiah's growl
of warning.

Rikki's body shook, and she pushed herself closer to
Jeremiah in a vain attempt to crawl inside him and warm
up. She knew it was left over psychic energy that was
causing the coldness, but it didn't stop her from clinging
to her mate. At least, she told herself that was the reason
why, and it had nothing to do with the lost eyes of a
woman who had put her life on the line several times for
others.

"Rikki." Angel's tone was patient, but Rikki could hear
the worry in it. "What happened?"

Jeremiah placed a gentle kiss on her temple, holding
her tightly. That was when she noticed she was still on the
ground, where she'd collapsed in the beginning of the
visions. Visions. More than one.

Lifting her head, she met her alpha mate's gaze. "My
gift has never worked like that before. There was so
much. So many visions from the past." A tear slid down
her cheek as she whispered, "Amber helped so many
people at the risk of her own life. That bastard beat her,
whipped her, but she still helped. She refused to give in to

him, refused to run from those who needed her. She stayed, knowing she would probably die a horrible death because of it." A low growl filled the area, and her gaze swung to Bane. "She's alive, Bane. And she's strong. Somehow, she connected with me. She's," Rikki hesitated, "she's in hell right now. But she's a fighter."

"Where?" he snarled, his hands clenching tightly into fists.

"Somewhere in Florida. She's not sure where."

A roar left Bane's throat and he turned, slamming a fist into the hood of the Porsche. Rikki's eyes widened in shock when the front of the car seemed to cave in.

"Shit," Flame whispered. "Hope you didn't need to take that car back, Jinx."

"Fuck the car," Jinx snarled, turning away from them.

"Jinx, where are you going?"

"Hunting."

"Not without me, you're not," Bane growled.

Jinx glanced back at him. "I need to find out what part of Florida Amber is in."

"I told you, get me near that bitch, and I will get the information we need."

"Bane, no!" Sapphire gasped. "Please."

Bane looked back at her, growling through gritted teeth, "What would you do if it were your mate, Sapphire? Leave him on his own, or do something about it?"

Sapphire was silent for a moment, then her gaze hardened. "We are coming with you," she told Jinx quietly.

"You will keep us informed." It was an order, one Angel expected to be obeyed. "Call us when you get a link on where that bitch is hiding her. We'll be there."

"All of us," Chase growled, his arm going around his

mate's waist. "Amber is one of mine. I claimed her as a White River Wolf. You call, we will be there."

Bane gave the alpha a short nod.

"Bane?" Rikki struggled to her feet, quickly closing the distance between them. Taking his hand in hers, she placed the wooden wolf in it. "I told her that you are coming for her. She knows you. Knows your wolf."

Bane's jaw hardened, and he nodded once, his hand closing tightly over the small wolf. "Thank you." Then, he, Sapphire, and Jinx walked away without another word.

Rikki watched them go, getting into Bane's truck and driving away, her heart hurting for the man. Jeremiah slipped a finger through the loop on her jeans and pulled her back against him, his arms going around her waist. Leaning into her mate, she grasped his hands tightly where they lay folded over her stomach. "Do you think he will be okay?"

"He will," Angel said, her eyes going glacier hard. "We won't have it any other way."

Rikki snuggled closer to Jeremiah, her eyes on where Bane had disappeared from sight. She knew what it was like to be separated from your mate. She wouldn't wish that on anyone. "No, we won't."

22

Ebony slipped up and over the wrought iron poor excuse of a security fence, and then quickly made her way across the lawn to the back of the mansion. It took her less than a minute to disarm the alarm on the back door and enter the house. In two minutes, she was through the kitchen, down a long hallway, and up the stairs making her way to the large master bedroom in the back. Drawing her Glock, she paused to listen at the closed door, then slowly pushed it open. Her gaze scanned the area, then went back to the couple in the bed, fast asleep, unaware that they would never wake again. Victoria Smelt and her husband weren't going to make it to the next morning.

Raising the gun, Ebony gritted her teeth and fired kill shots at both. No, they wouldn't rise to see the dawn, thanks to Gavin Denowsky and their little fuck session the day before. She not only managed to extract the Smelt's address from the man's mind, but also those of the other two head members of the organization. She had no desire to take them out, though. Not yet. She would only do so if her current plan backfired. She'd chosen Victoria on purpose. The woman was a viper, and Ebony knew there was no way she would let the others allow Ebony to share a place with them. Ebony also knew they would fill Victoria's position right away. They wouldn't settle on just anyone. It gave her time to prove her worth. Time for her to climb her way up the ladder, putting her in a higher position of power. Something that meant more to her than anything else.

Shoving her gun back in its holster, Ebony turned and walked away without a backward glance. She had things to do, shifters and psychics to acquire, her father's organization to rebuild. Some of his followers were having an issue with her being involved. She needed to fix that situation. Which meant more blood would be shed, more lives would be lost. She was okay with that.

Make sure and visit my website for information on all of my books, and to sign up for my Newsletter where you will receive all of the latest information on new releases, sales, and more!

Website: **http://www.dawnsullivanauthor.com/**

I would love to have you join my reader's group, Author Dawn Sullivan's Rebel Readers, so that we can hang out and chat, and where you will also get sneak peeks of cover reveals, read excerpts before anyone else, and more!

https://www.facebook.com/groups/AuthorDawnSulli vansRebelReaders/

Dawn Sullivan

ABOUT THE AUTHOR

Dawn Sullivan has a wonderful, supportive husband, and three beautiful children. She enjoys spending time with them, which normally involves some baseball, shooting hoops, taking walks, watching movies, and reading.

Her passion for reading began at a very young age and only grew over time. Whether she was bringing home a book from the library or sneaking one of her mother's romance novels to read by the light in the hallway when she was supposed to be sleeping, Dawn always had a book. She reads several different genres and subgenres, but Paranormal Romance and Romantic Suspense are her favorites.

Dawn has always made up stories of her own, and finally decided to start sharing them with others. She hopes everyone enjoys reading them as much as she enjoys writing them.

facebook.com/dawnsullivanauthor

twitter.com/dawn_author

instagram.com/dawn_sullivan_author

OTHER BOOKS BY DAWN SULLIVAN

RARE Series

Book 1 Nico's Heart

Book 2 Phoenix's Fate

Book 3 Trace's Temptation

Book 4 Saving Storm

Book 5 Angel's Destiny

Book 6 Jaxson's Justice

White River Wolves Series

Book 1 Josie's Miracle

Book 2 Slade's Desire

Book 3 Janie's Salvation

Book 4 Sable's Fire

Serenity Springs Series

Book 1 Tempting His Heart

Book 2 Healing Her Spirit

Book 3 Saving His Soul

Book 4 A Caldwell Wedding

Book 5 Keeping Her Trust

Chosen By Destiny

Book 1 Blayke

Made in the USA
Coppell, TX
19 August 2024

36163152R00105